HUNT THE MAN DOWN

"I ain't got nothin' against you!" Merril cried. He began to tremble violently. "I never done you no harm—"

"Shut up!" Cameron saw cattle coming around a bend in the trail, and above the muffled sound of their movement he suddenly heard horses and voices. He shoved Merril, reeling, into the brush. "One sound out of you," he said savagely, "and I'll come back and kill you!"

He flung himself into the saddle of the pinto as the riders appeared around the bend ahead of him. They were three of the raggedest, wildest, filthiest-looking trail bums he had ever seen. They reined in as they saw him, then as he went trotting toward them they came on again.

The lead rider had a red beard, and his hat, suspended by the thong around his neck, hung at his back, revealing a matted tangle of red hair. "Howdy," he called.

Cameron lifted a hand, then he edged the pinto off the trail as the three came up.

"Lookin' for that Injun, are you?" Red Beard asked.

"Been lookin'," Cameron said. "But I got no luck. I'm quittin'." He lifted a hand again and kicked the pinto on along the trail.

Then behind him he heard Merril Backus scream, and he wheeled his mount up into the brush, raking his heels along its flanks. But before the pinto had taken half a dozen strides he knew the horse didn't have it. He had the sick feeling he was doomed.

"It's Cameron!" Merril was screaming hoarsely. "Cameron! Cameron! Kill him!"

The Lone Gun

by Howard Rigsby

FAWCETT GOLD MEDAL • NEW YORK

THE LONE GUN

ISBN: 0-449-14005-9

14 13 12 11 10 9 8 7 6 5

Chapter One

Brooks was riding up ahead with Joe Wood when they came to the familiar rise in the land where the wagon road that led to Judge Kingston's ranch wound off through the brush. From there they could see the lights of the town on the plain above the river and their horses seemed to know that they were almost home. He and Joe let the horses break into a canter going down the far side of the rise and then almost at once he heard Mr. Tilton's voice booming in the darkness behind them.

"Brooks!" Mr. Tilton called. "You hold in. Hear?"

They had been riding off to one side of the road to escape the dust, but even so they could feel the white clay powder settling upon them as they reined in, for the curly mesquite grass that bordered the road had been chewed and broken by the hoofs of the north-bound herds.

Brooks had expected Mr. Tilton to yell at him and he knew Joe had too. Both of them knew everything the old man would ever say or do, and their silence now was like a comment. It was as if they had shrugged and said, "Oh, well—"

They sat their horses, smelling the soft September air, smelling the dry, tangy smell of the brush and looking ahead at the lights. Brooks tried to figure which light would be the Reverend Ben Silk's house and which light would be the church. It wasn't more than nine o'clock. If they had a Sunday-night supper after the prayer meeting at the church Mary Silk would still be there. She would hear them come riding up the street and she would come out on the porch of the church.

"I'll never trail with him again," Joe said. "You hear me say it, don't you?"

"To Denver and back I heard you," Brooks told him. It always made him uneasy to have people criticize Mr. Tilton in front of him.

"We could of got in Saturday," Joe went on. "We could of got in last night. You know that."

Brooks glanced back, and now he could see the others. He could see the hats and shoulders of the riders against the stars. There would be a moon pretty quick. In the moonlight Mary Silk would be able to see him.

"That afternoon we crossed the Red—" Joe's voice went on. "Makin' camp in the middle of the afternoon. Then holdin' us back today while he spoke prayers."

"Quit mournin'!" Brooks told him. "Can't you see them lights?" He felt like the horses now. He wanted to run.

"Ki-hoo!" Joe exclaimed softly. "It's goin' to take half the whisky in Texas to wash the trail dust from my throat."

Mr. Dave Tilton rode up and stopped and the riders with him stopped. The horses were snorting now and their ears were cocked toward the river and the lights. The two wranglers came up with the remuda. Then on the rise behind them Brooks could see a pinpoint of light as Jules took a drag on his Mexican-paper cigarette. He saw the pale shape of Jules's gray horse and the bulky outline of the pack horses behind him.

"Watch that cigarette!" Mr. Tilton called, and as Jules came on without replying he called again, "Wouldn't want to start a grass fire, would you?"

It seemed to those who waited that they had heard the old man say the same thing a thousand times in the past week. But now it was different. This was the last time most of them would hear him say it. And, as if in sudden realization of this, someone laughed, not really at the old man, but simply with relief.

"Now, gentlemen," Dave Tilton went on. "Let's come back into town the same way we left it—in good order. I don't want nobody running their animals or getting ahead. Brooks ought to know by now how it is with me. Brooks and me made trail trips before. We went up the Chisholm to Kansas City—how many times was it, Brooks?"

"Three times," said Brooks dutifully. Yes, he thought, he knew how it was. He could see the old man riding through the towns with his fine Spanish horse arching its neck and prancing, a gauntleted hand touching a hatbrim; the old man, acting like he was Sam Houston come to life, or the Almighty, Himself, having chosen to drive some ornery longhorns somewhere, acting like it was a privilege to a town to have him pass through it. Yes, Brooks thought—three times clear to the Missouri River and once up to Dodge; then Denver—and this last trip had been the worst. Mr. Tilton certainly wasn't improving any with age.

"We'll come back into town like Texas gentlemen should," Mr. Tilton said, and he turned his horse and took the lead.

"Just so you pay us off quick when we get there," someone in the rear muttered, and it was as if they all had said it. For until he paid them they were his. He could talk and they must listen. He could treat them as if they were children, looking down at them from the eminence of his years.

The others could quit, Brooks thought. The others always did, all but himself and Willie Swallowtail and now he began to wonder how he was going to make the break after five long years. When would it be best to tell the old man, and what would he say?

As they rode down toward the town, the three-quarter moon rose over the plain behind them and there were cicadas shrilling in the brush and when they came to the edge of the town they could smell the river and see the fireflies in the patches of ripe corn behind the houses. The town, like the burned ruin of the ranch out on the western road, was his past. The town was his image, his identity in the wilderness of land, a mixture of tragedy and happy times, of good and bad, and all of it irrevocably a part of him and of his nineteen years.

The old ones, the Texians, had come there first, after the victory at San Jacinto. They had taken their land grants

7

from the new republic up where the grass was thick and there were rich bottomlands along the river to plant their bags of San Jacinto corn. His own grandfather, Jack Cameron, had come—he and Mr. Tilton and some others that were dead. They had staked out ranches within a day's ride of the trading post and the fort. They had fought the Comanches and started herds by branding maverick cattle. They had organized Tilton county and established an identity on the plain—the old ones had, the Texians, and of the old ones now only Mr. Tilton remained.

Brooks watched him as they approached the stage junction, a military figure riding ahead of his men along the moonlit road, the foot-deep dust of the road rising like a mist about him as they came up to the stage office lights. At the stage junction the Dodge Trail ended and the old stage route to the west began; the Dodge trail, once it crossed the river, became known as the San Antonio road, while the western trail started its right-angled flight toward the Pecos as the main street of the town.

He was home—Tiltonville. The Sunday evening loungers in front of the stage office sat forward in their chairs. The old man touched his hat and his Spanish horse shied, skittering sideways in the dust.

The town woke to their coming and the voices began: "Welcome home, Mr. Tilton!" "How was the trip, sir?" "See you didn't bring none of them cows back with you."

Brooks was looking up the street toward the New Freedom Church and the church was ablaze with light. Sure enough, he thought, there had been a supper and he knew Mary Silk would still be there in the church. She would be helping the ladies to clean up.

The church door was open and there was a couple standing in the doorway as the riders came up the street. Brooks recognized the bulky figure of Sheriff Adam Lufkin and it was Mary Silk who was standing there in the doorway talking to the sheriff. The sheriff was a single man.

When the sheriff saw the riders he came over to the steps. Brooks saw Mary, one hand lifted to shield her eyes against the light, gazing out at them. He saw the white dress she wore, the outline of her figure, and as he rode abreast of the church he did just as he had decided he would do, he lifted his hat and he got Star, his grulla cutting horse, to prance a little, tired as he was.

"Mr. Tilton!" the sheriff called. "Welcome home, sir!"

"Good evening, Adam," Mr. Tilton replied, and his voice was as casual as if he hadn't been away at all. He allowed the Spanish horse to rear and he turned it while it was still on its hind legs. "You boys ride on to the pens," he told his men. "See that the remuda gets a feed, Brooks. Then those with a mind to can spread their bedrolls in the freighters' bunkhouse. I'll be along later for a word with you."

They saw the old man ride diagonally across the street. He passed before the lighted windows of the Trail Drivers' Hotel and turned down the lane between the hotel and Tilton's store; they knew he was going to his brother's. Syd Tilton ran the store and lived with his family in the house behind it. Syd was nearly twenty years younger than the old man.

The rest of them rode on down the street, past the plaza and the austere stone silhouette of the county courthouse. Then, with the light from the Buffalo House Saloon falling on the street and casting their shadows hugely ahead of them, they could smell the cattle pens and the hide and tallow works with its warehouse of baled buffalo hides. They could hear the soft notes of a guitar somewhere in the lower town and now the horses began to whinny again, smelling the mules in the pens and the hay in the sheds behind the pens.

"Ki-hoo!" Joe Wood yelled, and now that the old man was gone someone fired a shot into the air, the sound splitting the night, releasing them, and then they were galloping up to the pens while a Mexican hand ran out with a lantern and opened a gate.

Friends and acquaintances came drifting down from the street as they unsaddled and there were extra hands to help old Jules with the pack horses, others to help carry the bedrolls and the saddles up to the freighters' bunkhouse.

Brooks was the last to leave the corral. He washed in the trough and slapped the dust from his clothes and when he came into the bunkhouse everyone stopped talking for a minute while they loked to see who it was.

9

"What's keepin' the old man?" Joe Wood asked him. "Is he going to make us wait around here all night?"

"He'll be along," Brooks said.

"I want my pay," Joe said. He grinned at Brooks.

Brooks found his bedroll and sat down. "You'll get paid," he said.

"Three months wages—" said Tarrant Smith. "Brooks, you hear them golden eagles singin'? Man, we're goin' to tie on a real old wolly-booger tonight."

"Are we?" Brooks said. He acted as if it were news. He leaned back against the rough board wall while the voices went on around him. "Sure we are," he agreed. But even as he said it he thought of the Reverend Silk, the little man in the pulpit of the New Freedom Church, always preaching against the saloons, and he thought of the Reverend Silk's daughter, Mary. Then he thought of the cool beer running down his throat, and he just didn't know whether he would or he wouldn't. He only wished Mary's father wasn't a preacher. Maybe the Reverend Silk ought to ride up to Denver and back; maybe then he'd work up a thirst too. Maybe he ought to spend a couple of months on the trail with Mr. Tilton. An experience like that was enough to drive a man into the saloons.

Another figure appeared in the doorway. It was, Brooks saw, the newspaperman, Merril Backus, correspondent for the San Antonio papers and assistant to Preston Henderson, editor of the Tiltonville Bee.

"Welcome home, gents," Merril greeted them. He stepped into the light of the lanterns, a stooped young man with a flat northern voice, ferret-like brown eyes and a wispy mustache. He was wearing a flowered vest, his black Sunday pants and a California hat. There were fancy sleeve supporters on his shirt and he held a cigar in one soft printer's hand. He was, Brooks thought, like the smell of the river and the sight of the main street, he was just further evidence that they were really home.

"Well now," Merril went on, catching Brooks's eye, "you all got back with your hair, did you? I hear them say you trailed right up through Arapaho country."

"Good evenin', Merril," Brooks said. "You're just the one we all want to see. Now tell us, Merril—who's been getting born, or killed, or married lately around here?"

"Nobody you would know," said Merril. "Couple of freighters shot up the Buffalo House a while back, but not so good as you did once. The news is still all bad. Drought news. Everybody on edge over the coming election—tempers flaring, banks failing, railroads folding. Cattle is quoted at a penny in K.C. The big buffalo herds all kilt and the hunters broke and driftin' down the trails. Where'd Mr. Tilton sell his herd?"

"Denver," said Brooks. "To the army quartermaster there."

"How much did he get?"

"Eight a head."

"Eight dollars!" Merril Backus exclaimed. "I'm surprised he didn't bring 'em right back home."

"We asked them cattle," Tarrant Smith told him. "We gave them their choice. But they said they druther go to the pens than walk all that way back with Mr. Tilton."

"He made us go to church in Denver," Joe Wood said. "Then he doled us out two dollars a man."

Merril took a pencil from his vest and fished a pad of paper from a hip pocket. "Eight dollars a head," he said, and he wrote it down, squinting against the smoke of his cigar. "You see much buffalo?"

"Bones," said Brooks. "We saw plenty of bones." In his own short memory the life and death of the great herds was encompassed. He could remember his first trip up the Chisholm and the mile-wide swaths of shaggy backs streaming over the plains, a time when it seemed that, despite the constant thunder of the hunters' guns, the great, living sea of buffalo must always be there. Gazing at Merril now he knew he could never describe to anyone how he had felt trailing up the Llano Estacado two months before, with the bleaching rib cavities of the skeletons looking like some monstrous new growth sprung from the plain, like ghostly cities where by day only the gray wolves and the prairie dogs moved, where the coyotes came to mourn in the nights. Day after day they had ridden through the bones and he had felt that something final had happened in the land, that something was over, something else begun; and he had seen this feeling mirrored in Mr. Tilton's face.

11

"Indians?" asked Merril.

"Big camp of Kiowas up near the Canadian crossing," Brooks said. "Just sittin' around there waiting for the army to feed them. Saw Arapahos after we hit the Big Sandy—small hunting parties. They kept their distance." Speaking of Indians made him think of Willie Swallowtail. "How's Willie?" he asked. Then he heard somebody laugh. He saw the grins.

"Well now," Merril said. "Willie, he's just fine. I seen him in town a couple of times."

"Nobody stole Tilton ranch out from under his nose?" Tarrant Smith asked.

"Not that I heard of," Merril said.

Brooks didn't mind them making fun of Willie. He knew Willie better than they did. He knew Willie's wits might be a little scrambled, but he had also heard Willie talk to owls and seen him catch fish with his bare hands. There was a Willie Swallowtail the others didn't know, and that Willie and he were brothers. When they hit the trail Mr. Tilton always left Willie behind at the ranch, just so there'd be somebody to watch out for things. Willie was a wonderful shot and, if you didn't know him, that half Comanche, half white trapper face of his would be enough to scare the daylights out of you.

He sat there while the talk became general once more. He sat there studying the faces of the riders in the lantern light and, besides himself, only old Jules, Joe Wood and Tarrant Smith had been around Tiltonville long. The other hands were drifters, hired on that spring for the roundup and the trail drive, and he knew he would probably never see any of them again after they had been paid off and had their spree.

"Where is he?" Joe caught his eye. "What in hell is keeping that old man?"

Brooks didn't answer him. Joe knew as well as he did that Mr. Tilton must be in the store. The old man would have the big safe open, counting out their money. He sat and looked at Joe's blond beard, met the gaze of the impatient blue eyes, so ready to laugh, so ready to flame with anger. He remembered the night that spring when Joe had gotten them into the fight. And now instead of Joe's

12

face he saw the face of the hunter, the black-bearded stranger he and Joe had killed. He could see the man lying with his arms flung out in the sawdust on the Buffalo House floor.

Tarrant Smith nudged him and stood up. Tarrant had shaved his trail beard that morning and he was wearing a clean shirt. Where the beard had been his dark face looked startlingly pale. "I'm goin' over and lean my elbows on the bar," he told Brooks. "Why don't we all go? He can pay us off over there."

"You better wait," Brooks said. He still didn't know what he would do, whether he was going to drink some beer or not.

"Wait all night!" Joe was on his feet now too. "The hell with him. We got the pay coming—our credit's good."

There was suddenly a concerted movement to leave the freighters' bunkhouse, but Brooks remained where he was.

"You ain't comin'?" Joe asked him, turning at the door.

"No," Brooks said. "I'll wait for him here."

"You can tell him where he can find us," Joe said.

Brooks nodded. He listened to them all going on across the road, heading for the Buffalo House. He heard them joking in a bitter, angry way and cussing Mr. Tilton. And he didn't blame them. He'd had his fill of Mr. Tilton too.

Merril Backus had gone over to stand in the doorway. Across the room old Jules lay on his blankets. As Brooks glanced over at him Jules sat up. He gazed at Brooks a moment and said, "He'll be at the store I guess, huh?"

Brooks nodded at him. He watched Jules rub his fingers thoughtfully through his curly gray beard. He remembered when Jules had come riding out to the ranch three summers before on a sad black mare and had stayed on to cook, to keep chickens and feed the hogs. Nobody knew where Jules had come from, where he had been or what he had done before. The only thing anybody knew about Jules was that he could cook.

Merril Backus came back from the door. He picked up one of the lanterns and relit his cigar. "You know," he observed, "I don't think those boys show Mr. Tilton the proper respect." He was grinning.

"He sold our chuckwagon up there in Denver," Jules

13

said. "I got to ride all the way back here on a horse. I'm too old for that. Now I want my pay. I had enough of that old man's talk. Now I'm going to quit."

It was the longest speech Brooks had ever heard old Jules deliver, and the cook's words made him angry. Why in heaven's name, did Mr. Tilton have to treat his people the way he did? Now Jules was quitting. And when he himself quit there would be only Willie Swallowtail left out there at the ranch with the old man. And how could he ever do anything like that to Willie? To Willie or the old man?

"You just got to remember Mr. Tilton is a great public figure," Merril told Jules. He was grinning again. "Mr. Tilton was a hero and he pioneered this part of Texas and founded this town. Maybe you never heard it, but it's true. He was Sam Houston's right hand. And when he's dead we'll have to put up a statue of him, a nice one with a stone waterin' trough at the foot of it. How you think the old man would like to have that statue, Brooks? Will he want to be ridin' his horse, or countin' his money?"

Brooks sprang to his feet. "You don't know what you're talking about," he said. "Shut up, will you!" He stared at the pale face before him, saw it flush with color, saw the brown eyes gleam with sudden hate. "You came in here with the carpetbaggers," he told Merril. "You don't know anything about Texas or Mr. Tilton." He turned on his heel and went over to the door. He stood there, knowing he had made an enemy, and for no good reason. For a moment he remained there at the door trying to analyze his anger, then stepped out into the soft September night.

He knew now what was wrong with him—he was simply afraid that he wouldn't have the nerve to quit. He was mad at himself, because he could see himself out there at Tilton ranch tomorrow, when the last rider had come and gotten his gear and ridden off—when even old Jules had gone—he could see himself there alone with Mr. Tilton and Willie Swallowtail, just the three of them, but he couldn't see himself standing up to Mr. Tilton and telling him that he was leaving, he couldn't hear himself saying the words. He realized that he must tell Mr. Tilton now. He must tell

14

him while the heat was in him, while he could find the words. Yet even then he wasn't sure that he could do it.

Walking up from the pens he could hear them yelling in the Buffalo House across the street and he knew the big night had begun. As he turned the corner by the saddlery the moon cleared the steeple of the New Freedom Church and he saw that the church was dark, but down the street there was a light. The light shone through the windows of Syd Tilton's store, casting a pale, green glow on the walk. The blinds of the store would be drawn, of course, while Mr. Tilton had the big safe open in the back room, while Syd Tilton would be standing by, watching him as he counted out the money.

Half of my pay for five years, he thought; he can count out that too. Just then the toe of his right boot caught on a brick in a broken place in the walk and he could feel the sole that he had mended twice on the trail tear loose again from the upper leather. He had wanted to buy boots in Denver, but Mr. Tilton wouldn't let him have the money. "Wait till you get home," Mr. Tilton had told him. "Why spend with strangers, boy? Spend to home." And now, with the sole of the boot flapping clumsily as he went on, he was aware of a sudden, exhilarating feeling of certainty and resolve. He didn't have to be bitter or angry. He could talk to Mr. Tilton coolly now. He could say the words.

It was funny, he thought, how a little thing like tearing that boot sole loose again had given him the nerve he needed, how it had made him all at once so clear and positive in his mind.

Chapter Two

HE COULD NO LONGER HEAR the reveling voices in the Buffalo House. The street was quiet, then there was the scrape of a chair on the walk in front of the hotel, a murmur of talk. And there were voices deep in the store, back in Mr. Tilton's office.

He lifted a hand and pounded loudly on the heavy door, half turning as he waited, seeing the darkened church across the way, the plane trees in the little plaza, the courthouse, the jail, all etched in the moonlight, etched in his memory.

When he heard steps in the store he turned back. The door opened and Sheriff Lufkin stood there in the light. Whenever he saw Adam Lufkin, Brooks would think of the picture in the school book, a line drawing of a Roman gladiator. The sheriff wore his pants snug, in the fashion, and his legs were like the gladiator's, huge and heavy-muscled, like the trunks of two young oaks. He was still young, thirty perhaps, blond, with heavy sideburns and a thick mustache and, for a sheriff, he smiled a lot, but when he smiled his blue eyes remained pale and cold. He said now, "Well it's our Mr. Cameron, ain't it—home again." And with the words came the smile, but the eyes said, "I'll get you yet. I'm not forgetting last spring."

Brooks gazed at him, realizing that he didn't want to have his say to Mr. Tilton with him there. Then he heard Mr. Tilton's voice asking who it was.

"It's Cameron," the sheriff called.

"Well, let him come in," Mr. Tilton said evenly. "Let him come in."

The sheriff stepped aside and Brooks entered the store. There were two lamps lit, one sitting on the stove, another on the counter near the pickle barrel, and as Brooks crossed the oiled floor he could smell the compounded smell of the store, the ginger, the coffee beans, the kegs of sorghum and salt pork, the dried fish, the kerosene, the leather, the yard goods, the oilcloth. He could remember all the

16

times he had sat in the store, waiting for Mr. Tilton to get finished with his business so that they could ride back out to the ranch.

The overhead lamp was burning in the office and for a moment he stood there in the doorway holding his hat, stood there like the men who came to see Mr. Tilton on his days in town, waiting, hat in hand, to borrow money, to ask advice, or to pay off on a mortgage or a note.

There was a roll-top desk and a long oak table in the room, and beyond the table the big black safe, its door ajar. There were fancy scrolls painted on the safe as well as the name of the company in St. Louis that had made it. Mr. Tilton was seated at the table and in front of him were a dozen or more small stacks of gold eagles and double eagles. He had counted out the men's pay and now he was eating from an opened tin of Italian sardines and drinking a bottle of mineral water.

Brooks looked at the money and thought of his boots again. He didn't want the kind of boots Syd Tilton sold, the old Kansas City kind. He wanted the kind he had seen in Denver, Mexican boots from Santa Fe, boots with heels that would not slip through a stirrup.

"Hello, Brooks," Syd Tilton said. "Pretty good trip, I hear. No trouble, anyhow."

"No trouble," Brooks agreed. He glanced away from the stacked gold coins, looked at Syd who was sitting at the far end of the table. Syd was wearing a soft white shirt and a black string tie. Syd had a short gray beard and he was bald; he didn't look at all like Mr. Tilton. Mr. Tilton was taller and his gray hair was thick, growing in a mane that hung down over his collar. Mr. Tilton never put on a necktie and seldom a coat, but wore his cotton shirts with the collar buttoned at the throat. And he always wore a dark vest, with a heavy gold chain swinging between the two bottom pockets, the chain anchored in one pocket by a big gold watch and fastened inside the other pocket with a safety pin. Mr. Tilton's nose was bold and beaked, like a Comanche chief's, and his skin was like an old leather glove, his cheekbones high and broad. The slitted eyes that gazed out at you from beneath the tufted brows were very clear and very blue.

17

Behind Brooks, Adam Lufkin spoke. He was leaning against the edge of the desk with his thick arms folded across his chest, and it was clear to Brooks that he was resuming a conversation that had been interrupted when he had gone to answer the door. "It's dangerous for any man to be ridin' the trails these days on a good horse," he said. "They killed two men over on the western trail just last month. Took their horses and their saddles, their guns and their boots. You don't want to be ridin' around with all that money on you, sir. I tell you this country's changed. It's changed just since you been gone."

Mr. Tilton speared the last sardine in the tin with his pocket knife and ate it, then he put the knife away and wiped his lips with a bandanna. "Shucks!" he exclaimed. "Listen to him! Look here, mister, I been takin' good care of myself for most of seventy-two years. I been up and down more trails and I dealt with more bad-action hombres than you'll ever see. I charged Santa Anna's cannon at San Jacinto and I'm still here. I fought the Comanches all my life and I still got my hair. Yes, I can take care of myself. Time I can't, I reckon Brooks here'll be kind enough to shoot me. That right, Brooks?"

Brooks cleared his throat uncomfortably. "Anything you say." He was puzzled. Where did the sheriff think Mr. Tilton was going to ride with the money?

"I just wanted to make it clear I warned you," the sheriff said. "It's my duty."

"Thank you kindly," Mr. Tilton replied dryly. He glanced up at Brooks. "Where's the men? What did you come about?"

"They're waiting for their pay," Brooks said. "They're getting real ringy waiting. They're over at the Buffalo House now."

Mr. Tilton appeared to sit more stiffly in his chair. "The Buffalo House," he repeated. "Well now, it seems to me I told you I'd be along to talk to them at the freighters' bunkhouse."

Brooks shrugged. "I couldn't make them wait."

"I wanted to tell them I'm not going to keep any riders on this winter," Mr. Tilton continued. "I can't afford to drive cattle to market at eight dollars, and I ain't

18

going to do it. Till things get better I'm just going to sit tight. There'll still be you and me, old Jules and Willie. We can hold the place down for a while."

Brooks shook his head slowly, gazing at him. He started to tell him that Jules was quitting and that he was quitting too, then he realized he couldn't bring himself to say it in front of the sheriff and Syd. Instead he asked rather tautly, "Will you pay off here, sir? Do you want me to tell the men to come here?"

"No," Mr. Tilton declared. "I'm not going to pay anybody off on a Sunday. You ought to know better than that. I never conducted business on Sunday yet."

It took a moment for the sense of it to sink in, and even then Brooks didn't quite believe it. "Not going to pay off—" he echoed incredulously. Then he could feel his cheeks grow hot. He could feel his anger, as if it were the collective anger of all those who had endured Mr. Tilton to Denver and back, a fury unchecked now and flaming up in him at this outrageous whim of a tyrannical old man.

"I'll pay them out at the ranch in the morning," Mr. Tilton said, finally and authoritatively. He gazed at Brooks. "You tell them that."

"No!" Brooks exclaimed. "I'm not going to tell them anything. I'm not your errand boy! Not any more. And, while you're counting out that money, you can count out the pay you held back on me for the past five years!"

Even as the words passed his lips, he felt a sense of wonder that he should be speaking this way to Mr. Tilton, no matter what the provocation. And when he saw the old man's reaction he felt an acute sense of guilt; for Mr. Tilton was looking at him as if he had, suddenly and without warning, struck him in the face. The old man's eyes at first were wholly bewildered, then there was a look of mortal hurt. It had never occurred to him that Mr. Tilton could be hurt, and the knowledge that he had the power to do so and had used it goaded him, made him wild with shame. "I'm quitting!" he went on. "And so's old Jules. There isn't a rider in Texas that would sign on again with you. We've taken all we can stand. We're grown men, and you can't treat us like children."

"Stop!" Mr. Tilton thundered. For a moment he sat

there, not looking at Brooks any more but at his own work-scarred hands, looking as if someone had slipped a knife between his ribs. Then he said in a soft and somehow awful voice, "All right—you had your say. You can quit, and Jules too. Maybe I made a mistake, takin' you in when your own kin was killed in the fire. But I was friends all his life with your grandpa and I always treated you like my own."

The voice paused, and suddenly Brooks could no longer look at Mr. Tilton. Now he stood there staring hard at the little stacks of gold that glittered in the lamplight. Then the sheriff spoke behind him. The sheriff swore in a casual, jeering way and called him a bad name. And now Syd Tilton's face was no longer bland. His eyes were bright with dislike, with triumph, as if something he had wanted very much to happen was happening.

"I'll have your back pay ready for you," Mr. Tilton said. "I always kept half for you, like I told you I would. I tried to do right by you, boy. I figured you'd want to make a start for yourself some day."

Brooks swallowed. "I do." He swung abruptly and met Adam Lufkin's pale blue gaze. "Did you say something?"

"If it wasn't for Mr. Tilton here I'd still have you in jail for that shootin' last spring," Lufkin told him. "Or maybe I'd have your neck stretchin' a rope." He smiled his toothy, mirthless smile.

"Ungrateful trash!" Syd Tilton cried. "Your pa was nothing but trouble too—leavin' his family to go fight for the Rebs. Then comin' back here, talkin' trouble!"

Brooks turned to Syd. "You can shut up about him!" he said. Then Adam Lufkin grabbed his arms from behind, grabbed him just as if he were restraining him from committing some act of violence, as if Brooks were going to hit Syd or pull his gun on him.

Brooks struggled, but the sheriff's arms were thick and powerful, his fat fingers vicelike. Syd Tilton had jumped up from his chair. "Get him out of here!" He almost screamed it. Then he leveled a finger at Brooks. "Don't ever come in my place again!"

Lufkin twisted Brooks's left arm suddenly upward behind his back. He swung him around, laughing softly, and marched him out through the store. He got the door open, cuffed him on the side of the head with a clublike fist and flung him to the walk.

Brooks rolled, reaching for his gun, but he did not draw it. He saw Adam Lufkin crouched above him in the light, grinning, his own gun ready, just waiting for him to make a move, looking like a panther about to spring on a deer.

When Lufkin saw that he was not going to draw he straightened and spat. "So I got you right where I want you," he said softly. Then he laughed, turning back into the store.

The door slammed shut, the light was blotted out and there was the sound of the lock. Lying in the dust, Brooks felt suddenly quite cool and clear. He knew that Adam Lufkin must hate him so much because he also loved Mary Silk. As he got to his feet he remembered the sheriff on the church porch with her; he remembered the times he had seen the sheriff talking to her.

He stared now at the door he had been cast from and he knew the reason for Syd Tilton's behavior too. Syd hated him because he had hated his father; Syd's own brother had taken him in, and for five long years Syd had been forced to swallow his gall. Staring at the door he thought of the look that had been on Mr. Tilton's face, and his cold, reasoning fury became mingled with remorse. It wasn't that he disliked Mr. Tilton. It wasn't as if he wasn't loyal and grateful to him. If he could only have explained that. But now— He swung away, gazing across at the moonlit church with a sudden feeling of despair. What would Mary think? What would the town think?

After a moment he started walking slowly back toward the Buffalo House, with his torn boot sole flapping on the bricks, wondering how to tell the men, and now it was as it had been that night after the fire, with his father and his mother and his little sister suddenly gone from him. It was like that, when he had stood there in his nightshirt, sobbing by the embers of the house. He had the same bewildered sense of catastrophe and of injustice; he had the same numbed, lonely feeling. And all because he had been goaded to say something that was true and wanted saying, all because of a boot sole and the unpaid men.

21

Chapter Three

EVERYONE KNEW the men had pay coming, including big Jack Daniels, proprietor of the Buffalo House, and a good many were already drunk on credit by the time Brooks arrived. But when Brooks told what Mr. Tilton had said about not paying off until morning, and then paying out at the ranch, Jack Daniels cut off the drinks. He had thought Mr. Tilton would come and pay the men right there at the bar, and it wasn't until Brooks personally guaranteed to stand good for everything that he started serving the drinks again.

Then everybody really had a wonderful time cussing Mr. Tilton. They had thought the old skinflint had already pulled every ornery trick on them a man could pull, they said, but they just hadn't realized what a real talent for pure cussedness the miserable old rascal had. You really had to hand it to him, they said, this last trick topped them all. They went on to tell what they were going to say to Mr. Tilton when he did pay them off.

It was good that they were taking it that way, Brooks thought. It was the whisky that did it; he didn't know what would have happened if the drinks had been cut off. He stood there drinking whisky with them, but he didn't laugh and he didn't cuss Mr. Tilton personally. The more he drank the more unhappy he felt and the lower he got in his mind.

He didn't know what time it was when he decided to leave. He had gotten the idea to ride out to the ranch and wake up Willie Swallowtail and talk to him. He knew the sight of Willie's face would cheer him up, and Willie would understand everything; Willie would understand without being told. But when he turned away from the bar and started to take a step the floor of the Buffalo House tilted up to meet him. For a moment he lay there with his face in the sawdust wondering about it, then he saw how the room was rocking gently back and forth and when he saw that he shut his eyes and pretty soon he was asleep.

22

He woke while they were helping him into the bunk-house, and after he lay on his bedroll for a while his head cleared a little and he got up again. He found his saddle, hoisted it to his shoulder and went out. Down at the horse corral he ducked his head in the water trough and he rinsed his mouth, trying to get rid of the terrible whisky taste.

At the corral gate he whistled for Star, his grulla cutting horse, but Star didn't come to him and he guessed it was because his whistle didn't sound right, the way he was feeling. Finally, he had to unlimber his rope. He flung a loop into the dark, huddled mass of the remuda and hooked a black. Then he got his saddle on and rode out of there and by that time the moon was low and pale in the sky and as he left the town a cock woke and crowed.

The road to Tilton ranch wound along above the river and he and the black horse both knew that road by heart. The black was a night horse anyway and he put him to a steady lope, the pale ribbon of the road unrolling before them in the intense pre-dawn dark, while across the river a coyote howled at the fading moon. Just before the sun came up a soft spectral light flooded the plain, then it was dawn with the sun's first rays like a caress upon his face and in the dogwood and buckeye thickets the larks began to sing and the rabbits went scampering away up the gullies as the black horse passed.

Mr. Tilton, he knew, would already be out at the ranch. The old man would have caught a few hours' sleep at Syd's, the few hours that were all the sleep he ever seemed to need. Then he would have been up, by four o'clock at the latest, in the saddle and headed for the ranch. He wondered now what the old man would do without Jules. He supposed he would make Willie cook for him, and Willie would have to cut his hair. He could imagine Mr. Tilton sitting in the chair under the big pecan tree outside the kitchen while Willie cut his hair. He could see the two of them there at the ranch all alone and it made him feel bad to think about it, but it didn't make him feel bad enough to want to change his mind about leaving. He would just have to tell Mr. Tilton, real calm and nice this time, like he had always meant to tell him. He would say, "I figure to get married, sir. I aim to ask Mary Silk to be my wife. I want to go back to the old home place and build me a house out there."

Of course he was going to miss the ranch. He'd tell Mr. Tilton that. It had been a real home to him. And he was going to miss Mr. Tilton's yarning about the old times too, about how they had first come to the land. "Yes, sir—" Mr. Tilton would say. "We drew in across the river there, your grandpa Cameron and me. You know, boy, where I mean—on that little bluff there above the plum thickets. We drew in and there she lay right below us, the river, and chock full too; it was the springtime of that year, and I could see the crick runnin' down clear and the place where I figured right then I would build me a house. I could see the land rollin' back, with the mesquite green and blossomin', and the plain beyond, stretchin' far as a man could see. And there was mavericks grazing all along the bottoms in the rich grass, cows wilder than the deer, old mossyhorns that never knowed rope nor brand iron all their lives, just waitin' to be gathered into a herd."

Now in the direction of the ranch there was the sound of a shot. It came echoing faintly down the river, scattering his thought. That would probably be Willie's Spencer carbine, he decided. Willie would have knocked the head off a rabbit for Mr. Tilton's breakfast. Then he remembered how Mr. Tilton had been talking to him the day before as they rode along together, how Mr. Tilton had said as soon as he got back to the ranch, first thing he was going to do was to have Willie go down to the river and catch him a mess of them perch. Funny, he'd told Brooks, how his mouth had been watering all the way home for some perch. He guessed it was because of all the beef jerky he had eaten, not having a chuckwagon on the way home, and even running out of cornmeal and beans.

Now, remembering that about the fish, Brooks began to wonder a little about the shot. It stayed in his mind as he went on and as the sun climbed he began to sweat and he felt dizzy; he almost decided never to drink any of that whisky again.

He saw the horse and rider as they came out of the cottonwoods across the river, and he reined in. He watched the horse go racing up the path along the face of the bluffs, then he realized that the rider was Willie Swallowtail and he yelled at him, but Willie didn't turn his head. As the horse came to the top of the path Brooks drew his gun and fired into the air. Willie heard that and turned his head and he looked right at Brooks, saw Brooks waving his hat at him, but he didn't stop. To Brooks's amazement he just kicked his horse on and in a moment he had vanished beyond the rim of the bluffs.

"Well—" Brooks said aloud. "Willie! You act like you just seen a ghost or something!" He sat there a minute, staring at the place where Willie had disappeared, then he holstered his gun and urged the black horse on along the road. He was thoroughly bewildered by Willie's behavior; he couldn't think of anything that might make him act that way. Why had Willie crossed the river? Where had he been going? Then it occurred to him that maybe Willie had—like people always said he would—suddenly gone completely loco, gotten so excited over something that he had entirely lost his wits.

He dug his heels into the black, remembering the shot he had heard. And now a cloud had fallen upon the land and the birds in the brush were still. The only sound now was the sound of the black's pounding hoofs, dust muffled, as it raced along the road.

The Tilton ranch was on the year-round creek that ran down to the river. You came over a rise of ground, and the first thing you saw was the back of the adobe bunkhouse just beyond the stream. Below the bunkhouse were the horse corrals, the corn rick, the stable, the sheds, then the hog pen and the little house Willie Swallowtail had built for his chickens. Next to the chicken run was the weathered board-and-bat cabin Willie lived in.

The creek was lower than Brooks had ever seen it and he stopped the black halfway across. He made the horse stand in the shallow water for a minute, blowing; then he let him drink. He sat looking around him, listening. Down in one of the corrals Mr. Tilton's Spanish horse was eating a feed of corn. He could see the hogs moving in their pen, could hear the monotonous rooting sounds. He could see the chickens strutting in their run. It all seemed quite normal and peaceful, yet something was wrong. Over and over the familiar animal sounds there was that odd shocking silence. Something was wrong.

Across from the bunkhouse, beyond the big pecan tree, was the ranch house. The sun had turned the plaster on the thick adobe walls of the ranch house into a blend of mellow pastel shades, and the old cedar shakes on the roof had been bleached nearly white. Brooks felt a momentary relief when he saw the blurry column of heat rising from the kitchen chimney, and as he rode past the bunkhouse the sight of Mr. Tilton's chair beneath the pecan tree was also reassuring; then he saw Mr. Tilton, and for a moment it was as if the floor of the Buffalo House had suddenly come up to meet him again, jarring his eyeballs loose. Suddenly it was as if the whole world were tilting crazily, the ranch house, the sky, the tree. For in the thin gray shade between the tree and the kitchen door the old man lay on his back, his arms outflung, an opened straight-edge razor clutched in his right hand.

Scarcely knowing what he did, Brooks flung himself from his horse. He stood gazing down at the figure in the dust and for some reason he removed his hat. "Mr. Tilton—" he whispered, and after the sound of his voice the silence grew, seeming to expand unbearably about him. Then in the void he could hear the flies buzzing over by the kitchen door.

Mr. Tilton was in his undershirt. His shirt, gunbelt and vest were hanging on a peg by the mirror above the wash bench. He had finished shaving the left side of his face. On the right side the lather had dried and crusted like alkali dust on the stubble of his beard. There was a bruised hole in his forehead where the bullet had entered, and the blood had pooled and seeped into the dust beneath the gray head. The slitted eyes were half opened. They gazed steadily at Brooks, as if in mild reproach. Mr. Tilton looked almost as if he might be going to speak, but Brooks knew he wasn't—not ever—and for an instant the only thought in his mind was that now he was never going to be able to explain to Mr. Tilton how he really felt, how sorry he was about last night.

There was a fly on Mr. Tilton's face. The fly moved exploringly along one leathery cheekbone, then it mounted the great eminence of the nose and stood there rubbing its legs together. Brooks sank to his knees. He shooed the fly away and afterward got out his bandanna and covered Mr. Tilton's face.

When he rose there were tears stinging in his eyes and he just couldn't believe it was Mr. Tilton lying there; it all seemed a part of the night, of getting drunk. It was a part of the terrible way he felt this morning. Then he remembered Willie.

He stood there a moment longer, staring down toward the river. He looked at the bluffs where Willie had vanished, and then he turned and gazed up toward the brush-grown fold in the land from which the creek emerged. Finally he faced the house. He began moving toward the kitchen and as he went he drew his gun. Things were becoming clearer; he realized that Mr. Tilton didn't have his money belt on. He thought of the unpaid men.

There were coals in the cook range where a wood fire was dying, a slab of bacon and a bowl of cornmeal were on the table. There was coffee in the big pot on the back of the range. He looked in the oven and saw the burned biscuits. Then he went through the other rooms of the house, but the house was empty and there was a film of dust everywhere. He went back out through the kitchen and caught the reins of the black horse.

The door of Willie Swallowtail's cabin was ajar. He kicked it open and stood there with the gun. The cabin had a clay floor and there was a hole in the clay in the center of the room where Willie built his fires. Brooks glanced at the buffalo robe that was Willie's bed; then he went in and took the Spencer from its pegs. He sniffed the barrel, and it was clean, smelling of grease. He didn't know why he checked the gun; he never thought for a minute Willie had done it.

When he left the cabin he rode down through the cornfield to the edge of the trees and the trail that led to the river. It was in his mind that Willie had gone for those perch. He knew that Mr. Tilton had gotten the cornmeal out to dip the perch in. The old man must have made up that batch of biscuits and put coffee to boil and he was shaving while he waited for Willie to come back with the fish. That much seemed clear to Brooks.

The trail led down through the trees, through the willows and dogwood, and the smartweed was a burst of autumn color along the river bank. He saw the footprints in the mud near the pool where Willie fished, and some of the prints were not yet filled with the seeping water. Willie had been there.

On the way back toward the ranch house he rode slowly, using his eyes, and presently, beneath some brush he saw the gleam of the fish. There were three fat perch strung on a twig, and Willie's fishline was there too. From where he sat the black horse he could look up through the cornfield. He could see Mr. Tilton lying there. And now he knew that Willie, returning with the fish, had heard the shot, must also have seen who fired it. But at this point his understanding of Willie's behavior ceased. It became confusing just to speculate on it.

Only one fact stood out: a violent, unthinkable crime had been done, and the shock of it lay upon the land, even the birds struck dumb by the proportions of what had happened.

Mr. Tilton was dead. With the thought Brooks became aware of his own responsibility. He knew he must ride at once for town.

Chapter Four

BROOKS PONDERED in a wild, grief-stricken way as he rode. He could try to place himself there at the ranch when the killer came. If someone had been on the road ahead of him as he approached the ranch, he would have seen the dust. For miles—in this drought, on any well-defined trail—you could see a rider's dust. But he had seen no dust in any direction, only Willie's as he vanished beyond the rim of the bluffs. The thought made him rein in, and he knew then, or he thought he knew, how the killer had come and how he had left.

He put the black to a lope again, angling off from the road now toward the scrub oak and mesquite brush that marked the wash, a ragged depression in the plain, with only the tops of the trees and the taller brush showing, a low gray rampart in the haze of heat. For three quarters of the distance into town the wash roughly paralleled the road, running along a mile or so from the road until its course led it north. Riders took the trail along the wash only when they were hunting cattle or deer, for much of the trail was rocky, the brush thick.

There were cattle standing in the shade along the wash, others stretching their necks for the yellow blossoms of the manzanita. As he urged the black along the trail he saw fresh prints of a horse, prints dug deep and elongated, made by a running horse. He kicked the black into a run then, crouching low in the saddle and shielding his face as they went through the thickets. After two miles or more the horse was tiring. He slipped and almost fell among the rocks, then plunged through a thicket. There was a gray horse down there, sweat-drenched, lying on its side. At first he couldn't believe it when he saw the white marking on the gray horse's forehead. But the star was there. There was no mistake. It was his own horse, blood running from his nostrils, wind-broke, ridden to death.

He drew his gun and leaped down in helpless fury, starting for the thicket beyond the clearing. But he realized at once that no one was hiding there; if they were he would already be dead. He looked around then, searching for prints, and under a scrub oak he saw where another horse had been tied. The ground had been chewed by the hoofs of the horse that had been tethered there while the killer rode to the ranch and back on Star, and there was the chafing mark of a rope on the bar of the tree.

When he turned back to Star he saw that the grulla had his eyes open and was looking at him. He went over and for a moment he knelt. He spoke to the horse, listening to the dreadful breathing, then he straightened. He leveled the gun and pulled the trigger. Afterward he mounted the black and rode up out of the wash.

There was a dry, aching agony in his head, in his throat, in his heart, and he rode past the stage office with his hatbrim low, looking neither left nor right. There were wagons at the hitch rails, and in front of the courthouse he passed three riders from the trail outfit, strung out and looking much the worse for wear. They were heading for the ranch and, though he glanced at them, he did not speak. It could have been one of them, he thought, though he doubted it. He could not quite picture the man. After the riders had gone by he knew he should have stopped them, but he did not go after them. He turned beyond the courthouse and rode down along the hackberry-shaded lane to the jail.

As he tied the black horse Gail Bull appeared in the doorway of the sheriff's office and looked out at him. Gail Bull was like Willie Swallowtail, except that the Indian half of Gail Bull was Cherokee. Gail was the jailer, and when Judge Kingston's court was in session he was the bailiff too.

"Brooks!" Gail said. "Hello, stranger." His friendly gaze sharpened. "Somethin' wrong?"

Brooks went toward him. "Is the sheriff in?" His voice sounded dry and rasping, like paper tearing.

Gail nodded. "He's got a prisoner now. Talkin' to him."

"This won't wait."

Gail turned and called. "Ho, Sheriff! A customer here."

Brooks stepped past Gail into the room. The jail was built of stone and it was old, a hundred years old or more—part of the fort that had once been a northerly out-post of the Spanish domains. The windows of the sheriff's office were barred, the glass dirty and tinted by a procession of fierce summer suns. In the cool stone gloom Brooks could see the sheriff turned from his desk, his chair tilted back against the wall. Before him stood a Mexican, small, stoop-shouldered and humble, twisting his straw sombrero in his hands. "No, señor, I did not kill the calf," he said. He said it as if he had already said it many, many times.

The sheriff tilted forward, his eyes like two pale jewels as they rested on Brooks. He made a sign to Gail Bull and the jailer took the Mexican through the stone arch that led to the cell.

The sheriff was smiling. "Mr. Brooks Cameron," he said slowly. "Well, sir, it's a real honor to have you here, it is." He took a cigar from his vest and bit off the end. He put the cigar in his mouth, but he made no move to light it. He did not ask any questions. He just sat there looking at Brooks.

But this was bigger than personal differences, Brooks thought. He forgot the sheriff was a man who hated him. He forgot how he felt about the sheriff. This was the law; he spoke to a symbol; he spoke to the silver star on Adam Lufkin's vest. "Mr. Tilton's dead," he said. "Out at the ranch—somebody shot him dead."

He was right, it was bigger than their feelings. It was like the mountains of buffalo bones; something was finished, something was gone from the land. It was hard to grasp the import of the words, even for Brooks, who had spoken them. He saw Gail Bull now, standing beneath the stone arch, his mouth open.

The sheriff spoke softly. "Mr. Bull," he said. "Go fetch Tyree. Quick!"

Brooks moved over to the water bucket which stood on a bench against the wall. He took a drink from the dipper, then removed his hat and sat down on the bench, and now his head throbbed with a dull ache, and he felt drained of emotion, almost sick. Shifting his eyes, he saw the sheriff sitting sphinxlike, watching him.

Presently Tyree, the county prosecutor, came in. His

office was in the courthouse, only a dozen yards away. Gail Bull was behind him.

"Bring our horses around, Mr. Bull," Adam Lufkin said. "Mr. Tyree's and mine. After that go tell Gaines and Kergan to saddle up and get over here."

Mr. Tyree peered at Brooks, identifying him, then he turned to the sheriff. "That's shocking news, Adam. Is it true?"

The sheriff shrugged.

"Well, what's the story?" Tyree demanded.

"We'll get at that right now," the sheriff said. "I wanted you here, Chet." He got up and came over to stand by the prosecutor, looming over Brooks.

Brooks leaned the back of his head against the wall and gazed up at them. Tyree was a small, immaculate man in his middle thirties. His pale, clean-shaven face was wide and V-shaped and his expression was always one of steely alertness, as if he were just waiting for you to make a move so that he might show you how quickly and cleverly he could retaliate. Looking now at Tyree's face and then at the sheriff's, Brooks had a feeling that he shouldn't have come there. He had a feeling that he had made some terrible mistake.

"First," said the sheriff, "I want to tell you real quick what happened last night, Chet. This Cameron kid came into Syd Tilton's store, blood in his eye, spoilin' for trouble. I was there. He cussed out Mr. Tilton. Mind you! Mr. Tilton—the man who's been like a father to him—took him on, a homeless orphan. And he tried to draw on Syd." The sheriff's eyes flickered palely with a hot blue light. The eyes held Brooks's, seemed to hypnotize him. "I tossed him out of there!"

"You lie," Brooks said, almost choking on the words. "I didn't cuss Mr. Tilton! I never would. And I wasn't going to draw on Syd."

"I see," said Tyree. He smiled.

"Now he comes in here—says somebody's killed Mr. Tilton out at the ranch. Mr. Tilton was going to pay his trail drivers off out there, Chet. He had the gold on him."

Tyree stroked his chin. "I see." He gazed at Brooks. "Well," he snapped, "suppose you tell us all about it."

Brooks told them, dryly and painfully, stopping once to drink again from the dipper, his head throbbing. He went through it all, all there was of it. He came to the point where he had found his cutting horse, Star, and then there was no more to tell, and he sat there with his head against the wall, gazing up into their faces, and their faces were as hard and cold as the stones in the wall. In the silence he could hear Gail Bull bringing their horses up the lane.

"One point—" said Tyree gravely. "I gather you don't think Willie killed him."

Brooks shook his head in astonishment. "Willie? Why, no. Not Willie. Never. And, besides—who stole my horse?"

"Why did Willie run off that way, then?" Tyree demanded.

"I don't know," Brooks said. He realized now he should have taken out after Willie instead of coming here. Willie had been in a panic, that was all. "We've got to find him," he told them. He got to his feet. "Willie saw who did it, that's for sure."

"You and Willie—" the sheriff said slowly, watching him. "You're pretty good friends. In fact, you might say you're Willie's only friend. That right?"

"Willie never killed Mr. Tilton!"

"Maybe not," the sheriff agreed. He glanced at Tyree.

"Mr. Tilton have his money belt on when you found him?" Tyree asked.

Brooks said, "No."

"You know the belt? You've seen it?"

"Yes."

"What did it look like?"

"Buckskin belt—little pockets in it."

"Where did Mr. Tilton wear it?"

Brooks said, "Why, around his belly—under his shirt."

"And you say it wasn't on him when you found him? Is that right?"

"No," Brooks said. "I told you it wasn't on him."

The sheriff smiled. "Was it heavy?" he asked softly.

Brooks stared at him a long, dragging moment. "I'm goin' to find Willie," he said at last stiffly. "I think we're wastin' our time around here." He made a move to step

33

past Lufkin and then the sheriff still smiling, hit him in the mouth. As he sagged, the sheriff hit him again and Brooks felt the bench come up hard beneath him, he felt his head smash against the wall. He wasn't unconscious, but he couldn't lift his hands; and he knew when Lufkin took his gun away.

A dipperful of water struck him. He drew a sleeve across his face and when he opened his eyes he saw Tyree examining the gun. Lufkin grasped him by the shirt front and dragged him to his feet. "Now tell us the truth!" Lufkin said heavily.

Tyree's eyes moved from the gun. "He's still half drunk." He placed the gun on the sheriff's desk. "Let's lock this up," he suggested.

Lufkin shook Brooks. "Come clean with it," he told him. "Where were you going to meet your pal Willie? You gave Willie the money belt, didn't you? Tell us now. Tell us the truth, Cameron."

Brooks tasted the blood in his mouth. He shook his throbbing head. "I don't know what you mean."

"You killed Mr. Tilton!"

He could only shake his head again, appalled by the sheriff's words, by what was happening, feeling that he dreamed it.

"You went out there drunk and you killed him, but after it was done you realized we'd catch you. You had to think up a story."

Tyree straightened his black hat. He smoothed the lapels of his gray linen coat. "Let's be going," he said to Lufkin. He turned toward the door. "Gentlemen!" The way he said the word it was as condescending as a sneer.

Brooks saw that there were figures in the doorway, blotting out the hot noon light. Gail Bull stood there, his black eyes smouldering in a suddenly masklike face; and there were two fat deputies, Gaines and Kergan; then Merril Backus, like a ferret that had slipped into that cool stone place, come there eagerly, stealthily, scenting blood.

"I want to get it on the San Antonio wire," Merril told the prosecutor. He sounded breathless as if he had been running. "Is it true, Chet?" His eyes darted at Brooks. "What's going on here?"

34

Tyree frowned, grasping delicately at the lapels of his coat, looking as if he were in a courtroom. "All we got right now is this young fellow's story, Merril. He says he rode out to the ranch and found Mr. Tilton lying there, shot dead, money belt gone. Mr. Tilton was to pay his riders at the ranch today, and had all that gold on him."

Merril licked his lips, watching Brooks. "He do it, you figure?"

Tyree cleared his throat. "We're holding him," he declared. "That's all I can tell you at this time. We're holding this Brooks Cameron while we check his story. We're on our way out to Tilton ranch right now." He turned. "Ready, Sheriff?"

"Mr. Bull!" said Lufkin, and Gail Bull came over to him. "Open up the cell," Lufkin ordered. He swung Brooks around, and again he had the arm, forcing it upward.

It seemed to Brooks that until that moment he had lived all his life in blind innocence, believing in the essential goodness of men and the ultimate justice of the law. It was as if it had taken the pain that seared now through his twisted arm, and the black hole of the cell yawning before him, finally to open his eyes. He lashed back suddenly with his right boot, catching the sheriff on one shin. As Lufkin grunted, relaxing his grip a little, he wrenched free and lunged for the desk where his gun lay.

He took one step, no more, for Lufkin tripped him neatly and he heard the sheriff's mocking laughter as he fell. Then, catlike, Lufkin was on him, clubbing him with quick, cruel blows, dragging him to his feet once more with his bull strength, dragging him through the stone arch, across the corridor, into the cell. Now he was down again and a boot crashed against his ribs. He lay gasping in a sea of pain while the cell door closed. Then a key grated in a lock and there was a remote clanging of iron bolts.

Chapter Five

THE STONE BLOCKS of the cell floor had been worn smooth by a century of prisoners, by men in boots, in sandals, in moccasins, by men barefoot and bereft of hope, men caged in that gloom, with their eyes on the small, barred window through which they could see the blue Texas sky; Spaniards, Mexicans, Indians, men like himself, they had been. There were two buckets in the cell, a slop bucket and another one of water with a tin dipper chained to it, and there were two cornshuck pallets on the floor, and there was a bench. That was all the furnishings, and for ornament and occupation men had scratched their initials on the stones near the window, where it was possible to see, and someone else had laboriously carved a cross there. The cross was beautifully done, and to one in that cell a cross acquired meaning.

The little Mexican prayed before the cross, kneeling there beneath the window in the last golden light, and now Brooks could no longer hear the blacksmith's hammer, and there were no longer the shrill voices of the children who had been playing in the plaza. He heard a horse go up the lane, then the crickets began chirruping softly. It was evening, and he had not moved.

At the bottom of the cell door there was a space between the door and the floor, and some time earlier Gail Bull had pushed two tin plates through the opening. The plates were still there, the food on them untouched, for the Mexican had not eaten either. He could see the food now. There were two biscuits on each plate, a piece of beef, and some beans.

Someone struck a light in the sheriff's office. He could see the light beneath the door and through the slot higher up in the door. Steps approached and there was the gleam of an eye in the slot. "Brooks?" Gail Bull said.

Brooks did not answer, and after a moment the jailer knelt and pulled out the untouched plates. His eyes reappeared at the slot. "You didn't eat," he said. He waited a moment, then spoke again. "Me, I don't think you done it." After that he continued to stand there, looking in, waiting. "How you feelin'?" he asked finally.

Brooks sat up, grunting at the pain in his ribs. "I'm all right." He touched his swollen lips, feeling the dried blood.

"Just don't go fightin' with that sheriff again," Gail told him. "That won't get you nowhere—nowhere at all." He turned and went away.

Brooks got up and went to the water bucket. He drank, then tore a piece from his shirt tail, dipped it in the water and bathed his face. After that he sat on the bench and waited.

The two deputies, Gaines and Kergan, came for him. They stood there in the corridor, and it was as if he could read his fate in their dimly seen faces. They stood with guns drawn while Gail Bull unlocked the cell. Without saying a word to him they took him out through the sheriff's office and along the lane to the back of the courthouse. There were figures standing around the courthouse and he heard his name spoken, but the faces were a blur to him.

He glimpsed the crowd in front of the Trail Drivers' Hotel. Then they went through the rear door of the courthouse and the deputies urged him up the stairs. They still had their guns ready and each of them had hold of one of his arms. They held onto him as if he were some wild animal and, once inside the building, they both glanced at his face in the light and there was a chill, deathly look in their eyes.

Tyree and the sheriff were in the prosecutor's office. The deputies flung him into a chair by the prosecutor's desk and Tyree rose and tilted the green glass shade on his desk lamp so that the light fell on Brooks's face. Then Tyree leaned back against the desk while the sheriff sat on a small table swinging his dusty boots. The two deputies stood by the locked door, their jaws working slowly on their cuds, and for a while they all just stared at him.

"Tell us about it," Tyree said at last. "Tell us the truth now, and save us all a lot of trouble."

Brooks did not look at him, nor give a sign that he had heard him. He sat there staring at a steel engraving on the

37

wall. The engraving was of Governor Davis, the man his
father had hated so; Davis, king of the carpetbaggers, the
force behind Judge Kingston, Tyree and the sheriff, the
man who had taken away his father's vote, made outcasts
of all those who had fought for the South. It was as if the
portrait, with its cold, engraved eyes, had addressed him;
as if Davis, with all his autocratic power, were responsible
for this monstrous conspiracy.

The sheriff swung off the table and moved toward him.
Grinning faintly, he slapped Brooks's face. "You answer
Mr. Tyree when he speaks to you," he said. He slapped
him again several times, doing it almost casually, as if it
were just another job, rocking Brooks's head back and
forth, starting his torn lips to bleeding again.

Afterward Brooks sat and stared once more at the engraving. And now, with the blood running down his chin,
he understood his father as he never had before. He
recognized the helpless fury that must have been his, he
knew why his father had spoken out as he did, defying
them.

Tyree was talking to him again now. He was telling him
how he had ridden out to the ranch that morning and
murdered Mr. Tilton. Tyree was pacing slowly back and
forth spinning his story, and even to Brooks it sounded
almost as if it might have happened the way the prosecutor was telling it. It was like a dream, sitting there. It
was as if he had really done it. And he knew only Willie
Swallowtail could save him.

They came and took him from the cell again in the
morning. They took him before Judge Kingston and he
was arraigned, formally charged with the murder of Mr.
Tilton, and a date was set for his trial. The judge then
asked him if he knew anyone he wanted to act as his
lawyer. When Brooks shook his head the judge announced
that the court would appoint counsel. After that the deputies returned him to the cell.

When he got back, the little Mexican was gone and he
supposed they had taken him out to the judge's ranch.
That was the way they said the judge did; when he needed
another hand to help on the ranch the sheriff would ar-

rest a Mexican for something or other and the prisoner would serve out his sentence working on the ranch.

But they wouldn't give him ranch work, he thought. They would have a rope for him.

He ate some of the beans and beef that noon, and Gail Bull took his torn boot away to mend. There were voices in the sheriff's office all afternoon, but the heavy doors of the corridor arch were closed and he could not hear who was there or what was said. He lay on the cornshuck pallet and gazed up through the narrow cell window at the sky. He thought of Mary Silk, and to think of her hurt worse than his ribs did.

Mary's father, the Reverend Silk, had been a cowhand himself once, but he got the word and after that had ridden around Texas preaching, holding services in towns too small to have a church, at roundups, or wherever there was no regular ministry and he could get a few folks together to listen to him. The Reverend Silk had knocked around enough to have a healthy respect for the power and influence of the devil and, after listening to him on one of his good Sundays, people came out of his church with the feeling that what they had heard and witnessed was not so much a religious service as it was a rousing personal duel between Ben Silk and his long-time enemy, Satan.

A dozen years before he had picked Tiltonville as a place in need of saving, settling there with his wife and little girl, Mary, preaching in a tent the first summer, then building the New Freedom Church on land old Mr. Tilton gave him.

Brooks had been in love with Mary Silk ever since he first laid eyes on her, a black-haired little girl with blue eyes, lips red as cholla berries and a smile that made you wish she would smile all the time. They had gone to Tilton School together, and ever since he was a kid he had planned to ask her to be his wife. He would rebuild the old home place and marry her. That had been his dream, to build a house for Mary Silk on the land that had been his father's and his grandfather's, and to have cattle on that range bearing the old Bar-C brand.

He got up suddenly, pacing the cell, striding back and forth over the stones in his socks. He had to get out of there and find Willie. Once this was clear to him, he felt better. He sat down again and began turning the matter over in his mind.

"Gail," he said, when the jailer brought his supper, "I'm getting mightly lonesome in here. Can't you talk for a while?"

"I'll be back," Gail told him, and in a minute he returned. The key ground in the lock and he entered the cell. "Lufkin—" he said. "He wouldn't let me do this, but them deputies don't care." He closed the heavy door and came over and sat down on the cot. "You can't have no visitors."

"Where's Lufkin?"

"Out lookin' for Willie," Gail said. "He deputized Matt Hunter."

"Hunter?" The name, in an entirely different way, provoked as much awe as Mr. Tilton's had. Matt Hunter was old too. He had been a scout and a plainsman before he turned to skinning buffalo. He had led the first wagons through the high passes into California; he had trapped in the Rockies and lived with the Sioux.

Gail nodded. "Hunter been layin' around the Buffalo House. Out of work, like the rest of them skinners." Gail looked surprised. "Lufkin got Syd Tilton to put up a thousand dollars reward for Willie. Imagine that. For an Injun—practically an Injun, anyway, a plain half Comanche. A thousand dollars."

"A thousand dollars!" Brooks couldn't believe it.

Gail nodded. "It's the truth. Dead or alive."

"Dead! How's Willie goin' to tell what he seen if he's dead?"

"If anybody can find him Matt Hunter can."

"Willie ain't dangerous," Brooks said. "Why do they say dead or alive? Matt Hunter would kill him just to save himself trouble." He got up and paced over to the cell window. "Gail," he said, "I got to get out of here. I got to find Willie myself."

As he spoke the notes of a bugle drifted into the cell and Gail, ignoring what he had just heard him say, said, "There's the stage. Another load of folks for the funeral."

Brooks turned. "When is it?" In the hot weather he

would have thought Mr. Tilton would already have been buried.

"Tomorrow," Gail said. "Folks comin' from all over."

Brooks hesitated, then said, "Where is he?"

Gail looked up at him. "Mr. Tilton? They got him in the ice house over back of the hotel."

Brooks shook his head. Mr. Tilton wouldn't like that. But he would like a nice big funeral, a band playing maybe and people coming from all over. "Are they going to have a band?" he asked.

"I hear they are," Gail said. "A lot of speeches and preachin' in front of the courthouse, then they haul him back out to Tilton ranch and bury him there."

Brooks nodded. He knew Mr. Tilton would have approved. He paced slowly back to where Gail sat on the cot. "Gail," he said, and he waited until Gail looked up at him. "You knowed me all my life," he told him. "You know I didn't kill Mr. Tilton. And your own sister helped to raise Willie. You know it wasn't Willie done it. But Willie was there. Willie saw who it was. Gail, I got to get out of here. I got to find him."

Gail shook his head again. "Nobody ever escaped from here yet, they say. And they'd like it a lot to shoot you down if you tried."

"I'd rather get shot down tryin' than stretch a rope," Brooks said. "You know I got no chance at all at a trial."

"No," Gail agreed. "The judge, he'll appoint one of them—a Davis man—to defend you. They'll bring it up how your daddy was a big Reb. They'll make politics of it—if there's a trial."

It took a moment for the words to sink in, then Brooks repeated them slowly, watching Gail's face intently in the gloom. "If there's a trial?"

Gail Bull did not appear to hear him. He seemed to be listening to the freight wagon going past. They could hear the crack of the bull whip and the heavy voice of the mule driver. "Gee-haw! Move, ye sons!" And now, as the sun sank, the light in the cell faded.

"They're talkin' about somethin' else," Gail said, finally. "I was in the Buffalo House a while back to fetch the deputies some beer. Somebody's tryin' to heat folks up."

Brooks waited, watching Gail Bull's face.

"Lynch talk," Gail said. "Maybe it won't come to nothing. Not tonight, anyway. But they're sayin' you're a killer, Brooks. They're bringin' up that buffalo hunter you shot."

"It was either me shootin' him or standin' by and watch him shoot down Joe," Brooks said. "Joe drew on him, sure. But he was only going to spray a couple around his boots for what he said. When Joe's gun jammed, that hunter was just going to shoot him down. What would you do?"

"I guess anybody'd do like you done. But that doesn't change what they are sayin'. Sayin' you're a regular pistolero—just too fancy and quick with a gun."

"I ain't no pistolero," Brooks said. "And nobody's goin' to lynch me for somethin' I didn't do." He gazed steadily at Gail. "I got to have a chance," he told him quietly. "You got to help me, Gail." He waited. In the dusk he could see Gail's eyes watching him, but Gail said nothing. "You know that boot of mine?" he asked.

"I got it fixed," Gail said. "I forgot to bring it."

"Where is it?"

"There on my back stoop."

Brooks said, "I got to have a gun, Gail."

With the words Gail Bull stood up, as if what Brooks said scared him, and as he stood someone out in the sheriff's office shouted his name. "I got to go," he said. "They want more beer." He went out, locking the door.

Later in the night, the moon rose, and there were voices over in front of the Trail Drivers' Hotel. The voices sounded louder than they had the night before—some of them argumentative and angry. Lying there on the cot in the darkness it didn't seem real he was there, and when he heard the other voice he thought at first that he was imagining it, for the voice seemed to come from the walls.

After a moment he sprang up and dragged the bench over under the cell window. Standing on the bench he looked down through the bars, and he could see a figure on horseback next to the jail wall. If there had been more space between the bars he could have reached out and touched the rider's wide hat. The rider was Joe Wood.

Joe spoke in a hasty whisper. "They won't let nobody in to see you," he said. "None of your friends. We know you didn't do it, Brooks."

Brooks said, "They goin' to try to lynch me?"

"They're talkin'. And the ones that's talkin' are buyin' the drinks and tryin' to get everybody else riled up."

"Can you get me a gun?" Brooks asked.

"Gail told me," Joe said. "I just slipped my own gun into that boot of yours."

The thought of the gun made Brooks feel so good he couldn't think of anything to say to Joe, except to mumble his thanks. He couldn't tell Joe how it was to be locked up in a cell with the feeling that the whole state of Texas was against you, how it felt to lie there helpless on a cot and think about getting rope burns on your neck for something you didn't do. With the gun it would be different. With the gun he would get out of here alive, or get killed trying to get out. At least he wouldn't get hanged.

"I'll be back," Joe said. "Right now there's somebody else wants to talk to you. I'll keep watch while she's here."

She! He saw Joe slip off his horse and vanish in the trees, then another, smaller, figure detached itself from the dark mass of the trees, came over to the jail wall and moved along to the horse. It was Mary Silk. She got a foot in a stirrup and swung up to a seat on the saddle. Brooks saw her face in the moonlight, looking up at him through the bars; her eyes looked as if they were on fire.

"Brooks!" she whispered.

He succeeded in getting a hand halfway through the bars and she reached up and grasped it. Then he realized that her eyes looked that way because she was crying and this fact seemed as calamitous and shocking as anything that had happened so far. To have her cry was worse than being in jail. A fury rose in him, and at the core of the fury Adam Lufkin's face.

"It wasn't you," she said. "Even my father won't believe you done it."

"Don't you cry," Brooks told her softly.

She gripped his fingers. "They're telling the most terrible things. Saying you were drunk and threatened Mr. Tilton, and were going to shoot Syd. Saying you killed that buffalo hunter last spring without any reason at all."

"Please don't worry about me," he said. "I'll get out of this. I'm goin' to clear my name."

"I'm scared," she whispered. "Oh, I'm scared and sick about it all. I want to do something to help—and I don't know what to do. You in jail, and the papers saying you're a—a murderer. Brooks, how can people believe it? How can they be so unfair? It makes me sick of people. It makes me sick of the law. All I can think of is you in here."

He waited a while, listening to her crying, her face pressed against the stones. He held her hand, looking up at the harvest moon. "I was going to get all cleaned up and come by your place," he told her. "I was going to ask you to walk down along the river with me again, like we did the night before I left."

"Oh, Brooks—" she whispered. "I've been loving you so long—just waiting all through the summer for the day that you came home."

"I was going to quit Mr. Tilton," he said. "I got the money saved to build on the old home place and start to run some stock there." He paused. "All the way home," he went on, "I was thinking to ask you to marry me."

"I was just waiting," she whispered.

"I can't ask you now," he said. "It wouldn't be right."

Her fingers tightened again on his. "Brooks—were you ever to ask me, I can tell you now what the answer would be."

Now in his mind he could see her as she had been that other night down by the river. It had been June, with the katydids calling in the cottonwood trees and water murmuring along the bank. They had walked along slowly, their hands touching now and then and when they touched their awareness of each other would become so intense that they would fall silent. He had kissed her before, but it had never been like that last night. When he had finally taken her in his arms she had clung to him wildly and her lips had been warm and eager on his own. And, though he had always loved her, he had never known how

44

it could really be to love her, how it could feel to hold her and kiss her and know that she wanted and loved him.

"I've got nobody," he said gently. "No kin. Nobody but you. If you'll just believe in me—" He stopped then, with something in him freezing, his face pressed against the bars, listening.

"Lynch him!" a deep, angry voice over in front of the hotel was shouting. "Let's lynch the son, I say!"

He heard Mary gasp. Then there was a warning whistle from the trees and Joe Wood came running and seized the horse's bridle. Brooks didn't even have time to say good-by to her. Their fingers parted, he heard her sob, heard the choked, terrified way she uttered his name, then she and Joe and the horse were blotted out by the trees.

A moment later a deputy appeared. He came walking along the jail wall, carrying a rifle. For a while he stood at the corner of the building listening to the men over in front of the hotel, then he also vanished, the voices faded and the night was still.

Chapter Six

As the night passed the moon climbed, the hours hung like taffy on a stick, and still Gail Bull did not return with the boot. Brooks stood on the bench again for a long time, listening at the window, and tonight there were no late horsemen galloping home from the saloons, no shouted words of parting. It was as if the issue that had been argued earlier along the street had been decided, as if the entire town knew of the evil impending and now feigned a quiet sleep.

Around midnight a little wind rose, sweeping down from the northeast over the drought-baked plain. The wind started a high, harsh murmuring among the dry leaves of the hackberries; for a while it sent little puffs of dust through the cell window; then it died abruptly and again there was no sound at all in the town, not even the barking of a dog. He went to the cell door and listened, but he could not hear the deputies; if they were there they were neither talking nor moving around. Then there was a soft step on the stones of the corridor and a rustle at his door, and he knelt quickly and took the boot as it was passed through the slot. The boot was heavy and when he put his hand inside it his fingers curled around the smooth walnut shape of a gun butt.

He had friends. The knowledge was as reassuring and encouraging as the feel of the gun.

Now somewhere in the town a dog began to howl, began a mournful eerie baying at the moon, and as Brooks stood there listening he thought of Mr. Tilton lying over in the ice house back of the hotel; he felt the burden of his debt to the old man. Beyond and above his own present peril and the necessity of clearing himself, he knew that if he lived he was bound to bring Mr. Tilton's killer to justice.

Would they come for him tonight? In his mind he could see the riders moving stealthily along the dark dust-muffled streets to some rendezvous on the outskirts of the town. He could see the rope destined for his neck, the tree they would have chosen. He could see them wheeling their horses and starting for the jail.

He got down from the bench where he had been standing and went over to the door, and now he could hear the rumble of the deputies' voices. After a moment he picked up the tin water dipper and began to beat with it on the door. Presently the light of a lantern appeared in the slot in the door and there was the sound of boot heels approaching. The steps stopped at the door.

Brooks moved aside, holding the gun. "I'm sick," he said. "I need help. I got fever and chills."

A voice swore. "You go right ahead and die if you want to, Cameron."

"I need another blanket."

The deputy said, "They'll wrap you in one, boy, when they cut you down." Then he went away.

The light in the slot vanished and Brooks heard the heavy door that led from the sheriff's office to the corridor slam shut. He could make all the racket he wanted to now; they wouldn't hear him.

He began to pace and suddenly he wanted to beat at the stones with his fists, to tear at them with his fingernails. In the hills across the river a coyote began to talk and he stopped pacing to listen. Then he thought he heard the jingle of a bridle, the creak of a saddle and he sprang onto the bench to listen. There were horses coming along the lane from the north. As he watched, a masked rider emerged from the trees and spurred toward the front of the jail. Another rider appeared, then another. Brooks counted six more riders before he leaped from the bench and, with his heart pounding in his chest, crossed to the cell door.

Now he could hear a beating on the outer door of the sheriff's office and a muffled sound of voices. Presently there was a crash, the corridor door was flung open and booted feet came rushing toward his cell. He stepped back as the light of a lantern flared in the slot. He heard the key, then as the door was kicked open and a voice cried out his name, he fired. The sound of the shot slammed against the stones and the light exploded.

"Brooks!" Joe Woods's voice screamed. "Brooks—it's us!"

Brooks went suddenly limp with shock, appalled by the knowledge that in the next instant he might have killed one of them, then their hands were dragging at him and he was out of the cell and running down the corridor.

The deputy named Gaines was sprawled on the floor in the sheriff's office, lying on his back with his fat stomach sticking up. In the night outside the masked riders waited. There was a horse for him, a gray from the trail remuda. There was a rifle in the saddle scabbard, a gunbelt slung from the saddle horn. They rode back north along the lane, making no effort now at stealth, but with the horses running bunched until they reached the back street. There Joe grabbed at Brooks's reins and yelled at him, "Come with me!" They turned west while the rest of the group went riding on up through the pasture where Judge Kingston kept his milk cows.

They went west along the street, past the house where Gail Bull lived with his sister, Amanda, beyond the tallow works and the big hide warehouse, then they turned down to the western road, a broad ribbon of dust streaking along through the moonlight.

They traveled several miles along the road before Joe pulled in, and when they stopped Joe got down beside the road and lay full length with an ear to the ground. When he mounted again Brooks could see that he was grinning. "We beat 'em to it!" he said. "They had a lynch party set for three o'clock. That Gaines was right in on it, an' maybe Syd Tilton and the sheriff too. When they came for you Gaines was to put up a show of a fight, then roll over and play dead while they took you out. Tarrant heard them talkin' it over out in the back of the Buffalo House. They was to meet by that big cottonwood down on the river at the fording. They was going to string you up there."

Brooks's mind had cleared. "Joe—" he said. "Thanks. Thank Gail and Tarrant and the rest."

"You got a good chance to run for it now," Joe told him. "They won't be likely to try to pick up your trail till it's light. They'll have the telegraph wire hummin', though. You best head for the Border fast."

Brooks was gazing back along the road. "Tell Mary—" he said. "Tell her I'm comin' back."

Joe nodded. "There's meat and biscuit in them saddlebags," he said. "Take care, boy. Here—" He took off his hat and clapped it on Brooks's head. "You'll need that."

Brooks said to him, "I'll find Willie, and then I'm coming back." He put out a hand and found Joe's with a hard grip.

"Take care," Joe repeated. Then Brooks dug his heels into the gray's flanks and went on along the western road.

This land he knew even better than he had ever come to know the great expanse of Tilton ranch. He had ridden to school along this road, and when he came to one of the dry branches that the road crossed over he turned down it toward the river. After half an hour's ride he could see the eminence where their house had stood. He could see the blackened fireplace and part of the chimney, a forlorn stone pylon against the stars. There he crossed the river, onto his own land.

Some distance south of the river there was a range of wild, wooded hills. Into those hills his father had once tracked a panther, following the big cat's spoor along a cattle trail just after a spring rain. Deep in the hills they had killed the panther. They had skinned him out, then made camp for the night, roasting strips of the meat over the fire. He knew where he would hide out during the day. He was like the panther now, he thought. Only there had been no rain; they wouldn't track him.

Chapter Seven

WHEN HE WOKE he came awake all at once. The sun was directly overhead, the heat in the brush where he lay was like an oven, and the butt of the gun he had gripped in his sleep was slippery with his sweat. He lay there on the saddle blanket, not moving until he identified the sound that had awakened him. It was the gray gelding. He had tied it to a live oak tree near the little spring; there was some grass growing there and now the horse was trying to reach a clump from which the rope restrained him, and he had begun to paw the ground.

Brooks went over and drank from the spring, then he retied the gelding. After that he opened the saddlebags and laid their contents out on the blanket. There were some biscuits, salt, a piece of cooked beef, dry and black, a cloth sack of parched corn and a leather water bottle. There were also flint and steel and a piece of tow, a skinning knife, a tin cup, four dozen rounds of .30-caliber ammunition for the rifle and a box of cartridges for the .45. He ate one of the biscuits and a slice of the beef; then he put down a few handfuls of corn for the horse. It was time now, he realized, to do something, but first he got down on his knees; he bowed his head and thanked the Lord for his escape, even though he knew that the Lord might not have accomplished it without the help of his friends. But one of the things that Mr. Tilton had taught him was to try to keep on good terms with the Almighty. When something turned out right for you it didn't hurt to give thanks even though you might not be certain whether God had had anything to do with it or not.

When men got in trouble, they usually headed for the Border country, that vast no-man's-land of brush a few days' ride to the south. A man could exist down there in safety from the law until things cooled off, and then he could head for some place else. That was the sanctuary Joe Wood had automatically expected him to ride for, and the posse that would have set out from town after him also would expect that. They would watch all the trails leading south, and try to cut him off.

So much for him, he thought. But how about Willie? Would Willie head for the Border? Brooks just couldn't see Willie doing it. He knew Willie—Willie would get lonesome that far from Tiltonville. And, after all, Willie hadn't killed anybody, or anything bad like that. He'd just been scared out of his wits by what he had seen. He wondered now if Willie wasn't still hanging around, if maybe he wasn't holed up somewhere in the hills.

After a while he left the concealed pocket where the horse was. He took the rifle and wormed his way up through the scrub-oak and cedar to the top of the slope. He parted some buckeye branches and then, lying on his stomach, he could look out to the east along the river. In the distance he could see the town.

He could see the two flags on the courthouse, the Flag of the Republic and the Stars and Stripes, both at half mast and hanging listless in the heat, and there were two unbroken lines of wagons and carriages parked along the sides of the street, while the crowd stretched from the courthouse steps to the Trail Drivers' Hotel. When he saw all this and realized what was going on he took off his hat, and it gave him the weirdest feeling to be there watching it all in miniature; he felt as if he really were there attending Mr. Tilton's funeral. He could see the sun glint on the big brass horn, and it was as if he could hear the music of the band too. He could hear the voice of the Reverend Ben Silk shouting about the devil.

After a while the crowd began to break up. The miniature vehicles stirred and a column of dust climbed slowly in the pale hot sky above the town as the cortege began to move out toward old Mr. Tilton's last resting place at Tilton ranch. Once more Brooks remembered the old man telling of how he had first come there to the land; again he heard the words: "We drew in and there she lay right below us, the river—and I could see the crick runnin' down clear and the place where I figured right then I would build me a house."

For a long time he watched the dust column move eastward; then he crept back down the slope, pausing

51

occasionally to listen. The last time he stopped he knew something was wrong, for the birds, which during the day had become used to the presence of him and the horse, had fallen into a subdued chirruping. Then he heard something that froze him, the sound of an iron-shod hoof striking a stone. A moment later the faint sound of voices came drifting up to him from below. And now, from where he lay, he could see the gelding lift his head and cock his ears forward, hearing the other horses. For a moment the gray looked as if he might nicker, then he lowered his head again, stood once more in sleepy comfort in the shade, switching his tail with a lazy reflex at the flies.

The riders were coming from the west, following a fold in the hills, and soon Brooks could hear their voices clearly. Then, from where he lay, gazing out through the gray, dusty leaves of the oaks, he could see them. There were two of them. One was the deputy, Gaines, the other was the scout and buffalo skinner, Matt Hunter. They were riding along a narrow cattle trail, Matt Hunter in the lead, and where the trail forked, one branch winding down to the river and the other continuing south into the hills, Hunter reined in. He stared at the ground a moment, then dismounted.

Bob Gaines watched him. Gaines's heavy face was flushed and streaked with sweat. He took off his hat and ran a bandanna over his forehead and scrubbed at his kinky blond hair. Hunter untied a leather-covered water bottle from his saddle and sat down in the shade. He wore a battered hat with a thong under his chin, a soiled hickory shirt, buckskin leggings and moccasins. There was a Sharps .50 in his saddle scabbard, a bedroll tied on behind. Brooks scarcely breathed. Had Hunter seen something? He stared at the shrewd, lined face of the old scout with its scraggly beard looking like a growth of dead mesquite, the slitted gray eyes flickering at Gaines with a kind of indifferent contempt.

"Set a while," Hunter told him, and Gaines got down, looking very sour and gloomy.

Gaines took a swig from his own water bottle, then spat the mouthful out, retied the bottle on his saddlebag and stood with his hands on his hips staring off toward town.

After a moment he said, "Damn his lily-livered soul."

Hunter chuckled mirthlessly. "Sure now—" he said then in his rusty, drawling voice. "Who's gettin' the punishment here? Looks like it's me. I don't need you, boy. You think you're goin' to help me track down that breed? You can git, for all of me. Pack off on your own."

Gaines's flush deepened. "Lufkin told me to stay with you. You heard him."

"Why you reckon he did?"

"I'm no good at this tracking."

Hunter chuckled again. "Nor tendin' jail, neither."

Gaines said, "How'm I to know it was the wrong ones come for him? I just rolled over and played dead, like I was supposed to do."

"Set a while," Hunter repeated. He took a Mexican stogie from his shirt pocket, bit a piece off and began to chew slowly and thoughtfully on the black-leaved tobacco.

Gaines sat down. "What makes you figure that loco Indian's anywhere around here?"

"He ain't no Indian," Hunter said. "He's half white trapper. If he was all Comanche I could figure him even easier."

"Why you figure he's around here?"

"I got half a dozen reasons for thinkin' so," Hunter said. "Maybe a couple of 'em might be plain, even to you." He spat and for a moment seemed to gaze directly up at the place where Brooks lay hidden. "Suppose that ringy Cameron kid did kill the old man," he went on. "And, figurin' he'd get away with the killin', he give his breed friend that money belt. They'd arrange a place to meet each other, wouldn't they? It wouldn't be in St. Louie. It would be near—some place they both knew."

Gaines grunted. "Him and that Cameron—they'll meet on the Border," he said. "If they don't catch up with Cameron first."

"That's one reason I figure he's around here," Hunter said, acting as if Gaines had not spoken. "But it ain't my best reason for thinkin' so."

Gaines said, "How long you figure to keep looking."

"Till I find him and collect me that thousand-dollar reward."

Brooks was aware of the spiny little oak leaves biting through his shirt, but he did not move. He kept glancing at the horses that stood in the shade beyond the two men. Neither horse had nickered, but every so often one would cock its ears and look up the slope in the direction of the spring. He could hear every word the two men said, and now as Hunter, after a pause, went on talking, he watched his face. He wanted to see if he paid any attention to the horses.

"Care to know how I really got it figured?" Hunter asked Gaines.

"I'm listening," Gaines said gloomily. "I got nothing better to do."

"Why you think Lufkin made it so plain to both of us he wants that breed dead?" As Gaines shrugged, he went on. "I'll tell you why. Maybe Lufkin ain't too sure himself that Cameron is the guilty party. Suppose it was just some skinner drifting down the trails from the buffalo country that killed old man Tilton. Suppose that's what made that crazy breed hightail it out of there, fearing he'd be blamed." Brooks saw Hunter turn his head and stare at Gaines. "Wouldn't be no political angle in that, would there?"

"Hell," Gaines said, without much interest, "that Willie —he would never say it was Cameron done it, anyhow."

"That's why they want that breed dead," said Hunter. "This thing can win them the election in Tilton County."

"Maybe Willie did it."

Hunter nodded. "Another reason. If the breed did it that wouldn't win no election, neither. They want to keep it like it is, make out like the Rebs—and even the Reb's kids —is still tryin' to fight the war around here, murdering the leading citizens and actin' up against the law. I figure Lufkin sent you along with me so I could see you kept busy and didn't just lay up somewhere. I also figure he sent you along to watch me. He and Syd Tilton, the Judge, Tyree and all the rest of them don't want that Willie talking."

"What's the matter?" Gaines asked. "You want to catch him with your bare hands."

"No," Hunter said. "I killed plenty of others for nothin'.

And with that loco breed, killing's the only way. He's got to be stalked like a deer and killed like a deer. No man's ever goin' to creep up on him and surprise him."

Gaines was silent for a minute. "I still don't savvy how you figure he's around here," he said then.

"Well, if he ain't," Hunter told him drily, "I'll find it out."

"How about Cameron?" Gaines asked. "You think they'll catch him?"

Hunter spat his wad of tobacco at a rock and stood up. "If he rides at night," he said, "and hides during the day he ought to make it to the Border." As he spoke the sun vanished beyond the hills and for an instant the scout's pale, slitted eyes glanced up at the sky where the sun had been, then one of the horses neighed and the gray up by the spring answered.

Hunter did not appear to have heard anything. He caught his horse's reins and prepared to mount, but Gaines, who had also risen, caught him by the arm. "You hear that?" he asked. He was looking up the slope.

Brooks could just make out Hunter's words, heard him say fiercely, "You didn't hear nothin'! Come on!"

Then he knew that Hunter had also heard the horse, and he knew his present advantage would vanish just as soon as Hunter got out of his sight. Then he would be playing hide and seek with the two of them. "Stay like you are!" he yelled.

He watched Gaines and Hunter freeze and he called steadily, "Keep your backs to me, gents. Lift your hardware out careful and toss it over your shoulders."

He waited, his rifle sight grooved in on Hunter's back. "Hurry!" he prodded them. "Or you won't get the chance."

With his words the two pistols were drawn, made twin arcs and landed in the brush. "Now the rifles!" he told them. "Same way. And be careful, because I'm nervous."

As they reached for the rifle butts in their scabbards he kept his sights on Hunter. He saw Hunter's rifle come out and as it cleared the scabbard the lithe old scout wheeled, dived, and fired, locating Brooks's position so well just from hearing his voice that the slug from his heavy buffalo gun kicked up leaves near Brooks's right elbow. Brooks had

55

also fired and now he saw the scout lying prone near the rock he had sought to gain for cover. Hunter had dropped his rifle and he was making no effort to reach for it. He had been hit. He was holding onto his left arm, gazing up the slope with pale, expressionless eyes, searching for Brooks, or perhaps awaiting the next shot.

"Get up," Brooks called after a minute. He watched Hunter rise, and then he addressed Gaines who, having disposed of his rifle, had dodged behind his horse during the shooting. "You there, fatty—" Brooks told him. "Pull the saddles and bridles off them horses and start them toward the river."

While Gaines stripped the horses Hunter took off his neck cloth and wrapped it around his left arm. Gaines shooed the horses toward the river. The horses trotted a moment, tossing their heads, then began to lope along the cattle trail.

"Now you two git," Brooks said. "Head after them horses and don't look back." He knew they wouldn't catch the horses. The horses would run until they reached the river. They would drink, then cross and hightail it along the western road to town.

He watched Gaines lumbering along the trail after the scout and he could tell that Hunter wasn't badly hurt. All he needed to be dangerous again was his horse and his hardware. What chance would Willie, despite all his Indian guile, have against Hunter's cunning? What chance would he, himself, have? Even now, he thought as he went down to saddle the gray horse, Hunter would be guessing shrewdly at what he might do next; wise and old in the ways of animals and men, he would be thinking ahead, trying to anticipate him. It seemed even possible that Hunter would know that he had no intention of trying to reach the Border.

Chapter Eight

North of Tiltonville and the river was the mesquite-covered plain. South of the river, the northward hills followed the long, lazy bend the river made through Tilton County before turning toward the Gulf.

Brooks knew that the posse riders would have streamed through the hills that morning. By sundown they would be posted along the trails. Others would have ridden all day along the western road and would be turning south and east on the far side of the hills. If they did not catch him on the plain beyond the hills, some of them, he knew, would comb the hills, perhaps for a week; and then, he thought, they would give up, for it would be assumed that he had reached the Border. But Hunter wouldn't give up. Hunter would be there in the hills.

He hadn't intended to leave the spring until after dark; now, after what had happened, he had to leave fast. There was still an hour or so of daylight remaining when he rode out, and he knew the risk he ran; that the shots he and Hunter had fired might have been heard, and, in any event, it would only be a few hours until other riders, alerted by Gaines and Hunter, would be in the area hunting him. He left the spring and headed north, keeping to the flinty, trackless soil off the trail, going back the way he had come, heading in the one direction they would least expect him to go.

He rode slowly, stopping every so often to listen, and it was sundown by the time he reached the river. He waited there in the trees while a freighter went by over on the western road. By the time the freighter was out of sight the last light was gone and he let the gray pick his way down the slope into the river. He crossed the river at the same place he had crossed the night before, and rode back up to the road along the same sheltering wash. The moon had not yet risen and it was very dark when he crossed the road; he put the horse to an easy lope, heading northeast across the plain.

Before moonrise he had circled the town and was across the northern road. As the moon came up, he looked back. All he could see of the town was the steeple of the New Freedom Church rising from the plain. And now, to the south, between him and the river, were the rolling leagues of the Tilton ranch. Just below was the dry creek bed along which he had ridden after Mr. Tilton's killer, and as he went on the stench of his dead grulla hung in the night air.

On the bluffs across the river the coyotes had begun to call lonesomely, and he wondered if Willie were over there some place listening to them. The more he thought about it, the more certain he became that Willie was still somewhere in the hills. When there was trouble of any kind Willie had always made haste to get away from it. Then, when things quieted down, he would return. Unless he realized that he was being hunted, Willie would emerge from his hole some day and start riding back to the Tilton ranch.

When he came abreast of the creek that ran down past the house he saw the lamp shining through the trees. The lamp was in the kitchen of the house and he sat for a moment watching it. Who was there? Who, after the funeral, had remained at the Tilton ranch?

Presently he rode on, he went another mile or more before he turned down toward the river. There were cattle all along the river as he crossed, and when he got to the top of the bluffs and started along the trail he could hear cattle in the brush. He had chased cows up and down those hills and through the narrow canyons. He knew all the trails and he knew the springs. He knew the place he would hide.

Near a spring that welled up meagerly in a rocky fissure out of reach of cattle he unsaddled the gray. He gave the horse a slap on the rump and watched him trot back down the trail, then he hid the saddle and bridle in a thicket of mesquite. Loaded down with saddlebags, water bottle, rifle, blanket and rope he climbed up to the spring and filled the bottle, then he went on another fifty yards until he came to a thick growth of cedars. He forced his way through the low-growing branches until he came to a small open space. The moon was directly overhead now, and by its light he arranged his camp, then he pulled off his boots and lay down on his blanket with the fragrant cedar boughs over his head.

For a while he lay there, listening and thinking. He thought of Mary. He remembered the straight, proud way she walked, her fine, slender hands, so quick and sure. He remembered her lips that night by the river. He remembered her tears.

In the early morning he could hear the distant sound of an axe from the direction of the Tilton ranch. Birds sang in the brush, a cottontail flashed through the tiny clearing, and there were squirrels in the live oaks. Down below him he could hear cattle moving along toward the river, pausing to browse on the dry mesquite beans. He took a drink of water, ate a piece of the beef and went back to sleep.

When he woke again the sun was overhead. For a while he busied himself by taking the rifle apart and cleaning it. He cut a patch from his shirt tail and unbraided a length from the riata for a thong to pull the patch through the barrel, but he had no grease. He thought on that subject for a while, then decided to make a snare and catch himself a rabbit. He cut another length of rawhide from the riata. He soaked the two pieces in his water bottle and stretched them taut between two branches to get the kinks out of them. He spent most of the afternoon fashioning a snare, making it the way Willie had taught him to when they were kids.

At dusk he crept down to the spring and refilled his water bottle, and on his way back he set the snare, lying on his stomach in a thicket. As he returned to the cedars the sound of a rifle shot went rolling through the hills. He thought that somebody had just shot themselves a nice beef supper, probably some riders who were tired and hungry from hunting him all day. He visualized the fire they would build, he could almost smell the coffee, the chunks of beef roasting, the ribs and steaks.

In the morning, in the first pale light, he crept out to the thicket and found a fine, fat rabbit hanging in the snare.

59

He gathered some dead mesquite branches and returned to his hole in the cedars, but he didn't dare build a fire until the sun was well up; then, toward noon, over a tiny smokeless blaze of mesquite, he roasted the rabbit and tried out the fat in his tin cup.

The next day there were low-hanging clouds and it was misty and gloomy among the hills. He hoped it would rain. Even though he would be pretty miserable there under the cedars if it did rain, he hoped for it because of the drought. All day and all night now the gaunt cattle came drifting up from the baked plane toward the river. With the drought, and the cattle business the way it was, he thought, there would be plenty of riders with nothing better to do than to hunt for Willie and him. He thought of that thousand-dollar reward, and the more he thought about it the bigger it got. He guessed there were a lot who had known Willie well who would be out hunting him for that much money.

There was probably also a reward offered for him. And to think about this, to think of them out trying to hunt him down for money—maybe even some of his friends hunting him—made him feel like an animal on the run. And, with all that time to think things through, his hope diminished. Even if he did find Willie and Willie said that it was someone else that killed Mr. Tilton, who, besides himself, was going to believe it? All they would have to do was to ask Willie a few questions and he would get so twisted around that he wouldn't know what he was saying.

No, he had to find him just so he could tell him. Then he would have to carry it on from there.

But on that gloomy, overcast day, with the cattle bawling mournfully along the river and poor old Mr. Tilton lying in his grave over there, it seemed to him he might as well have said good-by to Mary and Tiltonville and all he held dear, and ridden for the Border.

Then, as that dismal afternoon wore away, he heard voices and he instantly forgot all else but survival. There were riders coming through the hills toward the river. He rolled in farther under the cedar and squinted down toward the trail. In the gray, misty light the riders looked ghostlike and strange. A huge, hunched man with a rifle held across the pommel of his saddle was in the lead, a figure Brooks instantly recognized. It was Adna Thorn, the Tiltonville blacksmith, and his helper Bill Ketch.

Brooks's first instinct when he saw them was one of relief. He wanted to sing out and say howdy, for they were old friends of his and he was lonesome. Then his jaw set, his grip tightened on the rifle and he moved a little, keeping the blacksmith in his sights. He didn't have any friends any more, he reminded himself. These men were hunting him—him or Willie, or both of them. They had only a golden reward on their mind. Two of the spotted hounds that were always lying around the blacksmith shop were ranging along through the brush and one of them flushed a covey of quail near where Brooks had hidden the saddle. The quail, like a round of buckshot, flew directly for the cedars and the dogs followed.

The quail started to light in the little clearing, but they took off again when Brooks kicked a foot at them. A moment later the dogs came bursting through the cedar branches. They rushed about for an instant, then stopped abruptly and stood peering at the cedar where Brooks lay. Brooks tore the piece of rabbit he had been saving into two pieces and threw it to them and they fell upon the morsels and gulped them down. Afterward they stood watching him, their tails wagging vaguely.

Down on the trail the blacksmith and his helper had reined in and were gazing around. They looked tired and dirty and disgusted.

"I reckon we wasted our time," Ketch said. "Likely to get our heads blown off to, what with all them trail bums out lookin'."

"They're not around here," Adna Thorn said with conviction. "Neither one is. I figure that Indian helped to spring Cameron from jail and they took off together."

Ketch said, "What about them riders this morning that said Cameron was seen in the hills over west?"

"Why wasn't they over there looking for him then?" Thorn asked shrewdly.

Presently the horses went on along the trail, with the

61

two men continuing to talk. Meanwhile, the hounds had dug up the entrails of the rabbit and gulped them down. They roamed the clearing with scavenging noses for a moment longer, then they took off after the horses. After that the gloom in the hills deepened rapidly and the air was damp and cool.

Chapter Nine

IN THE MORNING the sky was clear again, but Brooks felt feverish and his teeth were chattering. Then he became aware of the aching in his legs, and when he had struggled to sit up and pulled off his boots he saw the ticks imbedded in his flesh and he knew the cause of his fever. He cut the ticks out, then fell back exhausted, alternately dozing and waking, shivering and sweating.

Late in the afternoon he felt somewhat better. He had the energy to crawl over to the thicket, where he had snared the rabbit. He built a fire of mesquite twigs and brewed himself a cup of tea.

By evening he was hungry as a panther and his head was clear; he was uncertain only about the length of time he had been in the hills. By now, he thought, most of the searchers, like the blacksmith, must have given up. It was time now to look for Willie himself.

That night he left the cedars and started east, traveling by the light of the stars and what was left of the moon. The hills to the east were higher and more rugged and there were dense growths of hawthorn, cedar and live oak. He and Willie had hunted there. He knew the game trails, the hidden springs. . . .

For five days he searched through the hills, slipping like a ghost along the trails, fading through the trees, lying concealed on the crowns of the hills, waiting near the springs. He saw smoke, he heard shots and twice glimpsed riders in the distance. He guessed there must still be many riders in the hills, and on the afternoon of the sixth day of his search for Willie he had proof of it.

He had been lying holed up in a dense patch of brush most of the afternoon, because earlier that day riders had passed along the trail below him close enough for him to hear their voices. Late in the afternoon he emerged. He wanted to descend the hill, cross the narrow canyon at its foot and get part way up the slope on the other side before dark.

63

As he came to the trail he heard the sound of cattle coming along it. He listened a moment, then stepped out through the brush and the same instant a slanting shaft of sunlight cleared some tree limbs and struck the trail. If it hadn't been for the sudden brightness he didn't think the man who sat a stone's throw down the trail would have seen him. The man had dismounted from a pinto horse and was sitting on a rock smoking a cigar. He saw Brooks at the same instant Brooks saw and recognized him.

It was Merril Backus, and before the look of astonishment left Merril's face Brooks had drawn and could have shot him dead.

The meeting represented a catastrophe for him. He recognized that as he ran down the trail toward the newspaperman. Merril had dropped his cigar and risen. He was holding his hands above his head when Brooks reached him.

"I ain't lookin' for you," Merril said in a quaking voice. "I didn't even know you was around. I just rode in here to maybe get a story from some of the riders looking for Willie."

Brooks stared at him, biting his lip. He couldn't kill him. He couldn't do anything now but run.

"How are you, Brooks?" Merril croaked.

"Damn you!" Brooks told him savagely. He yanked Merril's gun from the holster and sailed it into the canyon.

"I ain't got nothing against you!" Merril cried. He began to tremble violently. "I never done you no harm. You got no call—"

"Shut up!" Brooks saw the cattle coming around a bend in the trail, and above the muffled sound of their movement he suddenly heard horses and voices. He gave Merril a shove that sent him reeling into the brush. "One sound out of you," he told him, "and I'll come back and kill you!"

He had just time to fling himself into the saddle of the pinto as the riders appeared around the bend ahead of him. There were three, and he knew none of them; they were three of the raggedest, wildest, filthiest-looking trail bums he had ever seen. They reined in as they saw him, then as he went trotting toward them they came on again.

The lead rider had a red beard, and his hat, suspended by the thong around his neck, hung at his back, revealing a matted tangle of red hair. "Howdy," he called.

Brooks lifted a hand, then he edged the pinto off the trail as the three came up.

"Lookin' for that Injun, are you?" Red Beard asked.

"Been lookin'," Brooks said. "But I got no luck. I'm quittin'." He lifted a hand again and kicked the pinto on along the trail. Then behind him he heard Merril Backus scream and he wheeled his mount up into the brush, raking his heels along its flanks, but before the pinto had taken a half dozen strides he knew the horse didn't have it; he had the sick feeling he was doomed.

"It's Cameron!" Merril was screaming hoarsely. "Cameron! Kill him!"

The brush tore at his legs and the pinto was no brush-popper, but when they came out of the brush he ran well sheerly out of fright. They were in a clearing and now without the sound of his own passage through the brush Brooks could hear someone crashing along off to his right and another horse was coming directly behind him. As he got to the far side of the clearing there was a ripping sound in the air near his head and he heard the crash of a rifle.

He hauled the pinto in so hard it went up with him and as it reared he fired at the man behind him. It was Red Beard, riding down on him like a buffalo hunter riding down on a wounded bull. The big gun crashed again and the pinto squealed and went back over, falling, toppling with him even as he emptied his gun. He hit the rocks and rolled, sprang up in time to catch the bridle of the lunging horse Red Beard had been riding, while Red Beard himself lay crumpled and still.

The horse was a big, shaggy roan, and as soon as he was in the saddle he knew he was well mounted; this was a brush horse, a buffalo horse, strong, rugged and fast. The roan took him up a winding, rocky weal through the brush.

The two remaining riders, drawn to the clearing by the firing, were now coming along behind him and as he reached the crest of the hill, a bullet whipped through the branches. There were several wild shots, then he was plunging down the south slope of the hill.

He knew the hills, he knew the trail; that was his advantage. But he also knew that every rider within earshot of the firing would be converging on the area. Within a few hours word of his presence would have spread; some time that night the news would reach Tiltonville. Then every rider in the county would be out hunting him.

Going down the slope, he knew that his only real chance lay to the south. By now the sun had dropped behind the hills, but there would be another two hours of soft evening light. He knew the trails, and with the powerful roan beneath him he could be almost out of the hills by nightfall, out of the hills and on the plain, with the whole night ahead of him to ride, a night's advantage over the fresh horses that would set out after him in the morning.

When he hit the cattle trail at the foot of the slope the roan stretched out, then the trail dipped into a canyon and coming up on the far side he was under fire again. A slug ricocheted from the stones beside the trail and a lead fragment, like a white-hot poker, seared his left hand. The roan gained the cover of some trees, then on a switchback of the trail, high on the slope on the other side of the canyon, he caught a glimpse of more riders—three of them. Just as he saw them they saw him and they reined in, whipping their rifles from the scabbards. As he wheeled the roan up into the brush once more, he heard the snapping of slugs around him, and the hills reverberated with the thunder of the guns.

The three riders continued firing until he reached a dry watercourse that angled down the hillside. Following it he had some cover, and the sound of the guns stopped. Then he could hear the men shouting behind him. He could hear horses crashing up through the brush.

He followed the watercourse around to the south flank of the hill, leaving it for one of the innumerable cattle trails. He followed that, keeping the roan at a perilous, breakneck run until he came once more to one of the main trails, the one he wanted to stay on, the trail

66

that wound south through the hills to meet the San Antonio road.

When he came to the trail he pulled the roan in and let him blow. And now he could hear horses high on the hill behind him, but there was no sound along the trail. After a moment he went on, putting the horse to an easy lope. Dusk was falling in the canyon now, and with night coming and astride that horse, he felt he had a chance.

Shortly after dark he saw a glow of light ahead and he turned off the trail up into the brush again. Later, he looked down from a hilltop and saw the silhouettes of men around a fire. The stars were out by then and from the hill he could glimpse the pale shimmer of the plain beyond the hills.

What moon there was, was high in the sky as he came out into the plain. He crossed the dusty gash of the San Antonio road and pointed the roan's nose toward the Southern Cross.

Chapter Ten

ALL NIGHT HE PASSED CATTLE grazing on the mesquite, moving north over the baked plain. At dawn he turned west toward a range of low-lying hills that appeared to stretch like a long, outthrust arm toward the south.

By the time he reached the hills the sun was high and a fierce, hot wind had sprung up. The wind tore the soil from around the roots of the dead grass that was the food of the plain, and the dust made a haze over the hills, and everywhere there were gaunt, longhorned specters moving north.

The hills, but for the scrub mesquite, were barren, yet there was concealment among them; the trail wound south through draws and washes, and where it passed over a crest and he would be outlined against the sky, he detoured around the foot of the hills.

The roan was tiring, and toward noon he stopped him at a sump where water lay in the alkali-crusted bottom of a dry creek. There were cattle lying in the water and there was a stench of carcasses further up the draw, and as they came down the trail toward the sump several vultures, too gorged to fly, waddled off into the brush. The roan drank and afterward Brooks loosened the saddle cinch and took the bit out of his mouth.

There was a pinnacle of limestone above the draw and, leaving the horse to graze on the mesquite tops, he climbed up there. From the rock he could see back along the plain to the hills of Tilton County. He lay on the rock with his hat tilted forward, his hands cupped around his eyes, studying every speck that moved in the noonday glitter. At first he thought the black dots might be cattle; then, as they reached a hilltop, he realized they were horses and riders. They too were coming down the spine of the hills, and even at that distance he could tell they were coming fast.

The chance he had was almost a matter of arithmetic and the durability of the roan horse. He guessed that the riders he saw were almost certainly a posse from Tiltonville and they would have come down the San Antonio road. They would have come fast all the way, while he had been trying to pace the roan, to save him. He figured the riders were now only about an hour and a half behind him, and it was time now to see what the roan could do.

Going on, he let the roan out again, but it became necessary more frequently to leave the trail in order to avoid the crests of the hills. After an hour or so he came to a place where he either had to keep on along an ascending hogback that fell off steeply on either side, or ride out onto the plain. He lost several precious minutes hesitating, then urged the horse down a shale embankment onto the plain.

As he raced along toward the cut where he could pick up the trail again he looked back and saw the riders, easily recognizable this time as horses and men. They were on a crest behind him, and by the way the horses were all spurting forward he knew he had been seen.

There was no point in trying for concealment now. If he could have made better time on the plain he would have kept to it, but by now the plain had become a rocky, broken waste. In the far distance, though, he could see the brush and he knew the Nueces was there. If only he could reach the river and the brush, he might have a chance.

The hogback had been like the hand at the end of a long arm of the hills, and beyond the hogback, like pebbles the hand had flung, were a series of buttes and rocky knolls over and around which the trail wound, to dip finally into a dry, narrow canyon that ran along for several miles, its rocks and brush whitened with alkali dust. In the canyon he could let the roan out, and he did, the big, sure-footed horse running well, appearing to have power and endurance to spare.

When the canyon ended there were no more hills, nothing but the rocky, cactus-grown plain, with occasional growths of chaparral standing out like islands in the barrenness. When he came out of the canyon he kept looking back, and when the riders finally appeared they were widely separated. Only four horses had held their own with the roan. The others had faded. But now, instead of appearing closer, the shimmering blue line of brush ahead seemed to recede as he rode toward it. The afternoon was wearing on, the roan was tiring. Still three of the following horses hung on. The fourth horse had stopped and was standing head down, its legs splayed out. The rider had dismounted. He had his rifle to his shoulder and after a moment Brooks heard the sound of the shot, but the bullet came nowhere near him. Then the roan stumbled, recovered and lurched into some stones beside the trail, only to stumble once more and plunge to his knees.

Brooks fell hard, and lay a moment stunned and windless. When he scrambled to his feet he saw that the roan's knees were bleeding. And now as he mounted again, the three remaining riders began to fire. They were, at that point, close enough to be recognized and he saw that the rider in the lead was Adam Lufkin.

For a moment then his hate was like a haze before his eyes, a swirling mist in which there was only Lufkin's heavy face. As he urged the roan on he drew his gun and snapped a shot through the haze. And still, even as he squeezed the trigger, he moved the muzzle of the pistol skyward. He knew he couldn't kill Lufkin, for to do so would outlaw him forever. He knew he could never go back to Tiltonville if he did.

The roan, as if in apology for his misstep, was running well again and in the next hour they gained a little ground. The sun was low and now the barrier of brush ahead no longer looked as if it might be an illusion; it had taken on shape, dimension and color and as he rode on the clumps of chaparral became more frequent and the stones and thorn gave way to a flinty, alluvial soil. The river, was close; he could smell it and he knew the roan could smell it too, and when the trail straightened out the roan called on his last reserve of strength.

But the three riders behind hung on, and as the brush loomed closer they began to fire at him again. Then he left the trail and began to dodge and weave among the clumps of chaparral and all around him the slugs came ripping through the brush. As the brush grew thicker he wheeled the roan down an open channel running off at right angles to their passage, thinking he had a chance of escape there. But almost at once, as they came full tilt around a bend, a deep wash lay before them, and even as the roan gathered himself for the leap Brooks knew he would never make it.

The horse was in the air, plunging outward and downward as he rolled clear of the saddle; then in an instant something burst in his head and he sank slowly into a lonesome, throbbing black nothingness that contained all his weariness and pain.

When he opened his eyes he was still in the throbbing void. But he could smell the brush all about him and after a while he stretched out a hand, groping, and felt the horse, and it was another little while before he realized that the fine roan was dead and could remember what had happened. It was night. He could hear the faint ripple of a river, and cattle bawling. When he moved again pain stabbed him, and after that he lay still; he shut his eyes and returned to the void.

It was dawn when he opened his eyes again. The birds were singing in the brush and he could look up through interlacing branches to glimpse a soft, rose-colored sky. Then, in the distance across the river, the guns began, and intermittently all morning long he heard them.

He and the roan had dropped about fifteen feet, crashing down into a growth of chaparral, lying there as completely hidden as if they had fallen into a well. He had escaped just as completely, he realized, as if he had crossed the Bravo into Mexico, which by now he knew Lufkin must figure he was well on his way to doing.

Although he ached all over, the pain seemed centered in his left shoulder, but he could feel no broken bones there. And there was also a lump on his head, and his face felt stiff and masklike with dried blood. During the morning he managed to get the water bottle off the saddle and drink, and he found some jerky in the saddlebags. He lay there all day, listening to the sporadic sound of the guns. Toward evening he crawled up out of the wash and made his way down to the river.

He bathed in the river, lying for a long time in the warm, brackish water. Afterward he crawled into a thicket

71

and slept, and in the morning he crossed the river and started walking south through the brush toward the sound of the guns. He knew what the guns were; the buffalo hunters, who had drifted down from Indian Territory, were killing the cattle for their hides.

Toward noon the brush thinned. Ahead, he saw that there were great open stretches of dead grass among the forest of the brush. In these clearings the longhorned carcasses lay everywhere, while gorging vultures sat in rows along the rib cavities and the air reeked of rotting flesh. The guns were close now, and he worked his way around the clearing, keeping to the brush. On the west end of the clearing he came to several fresh kills. He could tell from the notched ears that the hides had borne brands, and as he cut strips from one of the carcasses he saw the cuplike notch the old Bar-C had used. The steer had been an ancient mossyhorn, and he knew his own father must have put the brand on his hide and notched him. He was eating his own meat, he thought. He went well back into the brush with the meat, got out his flint, steel and tow and kindled a little fire.

By dusk he had worked his way around that clearing and come to another, and he had glimpsed two skinners leading a horse loaded with hides. As night fell he saw the skinners' fire, and next morning he watched them riding out. They went out in pairs, each pair with a pack horse to carry back the hides they would take during the day.

The skinners' camp was in the clearing at the edge of the brush, and because of all the cattle trails converging at that point he guessed at the presence of a water hole in the brush behind the camp. There were hides spread out all around the camp and there were several lean-tos made of hides and a pole corral in which two saddled horses stood.

Two men remained at the camp. They were hauling hides from a pile and stretching them out in the sun, not working too hard at it, but stopping now and then to argue about something and knocking off once to go and sit in the shade of one of the lean-tos and have a smoke. One of the men was a giant with a curly blond beard. The other was small and dark and wore a gun strapped low on his right thigh. The big man had no sidearm, only a long skinning knife hanging in a sheath from his belt, but there was a rifle leaning against a dead tree near the still-smoking breakfast fire.

Brooks started making his way through the brush, working carefully around toward the camp. Behind the camp a spring seeped down from the bank of a dry creek into a hole which the skinners had dug out and enlarged. As he filled his water bottle he heard the guns begin, and the sound was what he had been waiting for. The skinners, he figured, would start their work as far off from the camp as they intended to go that day and then would work back toward the camp.

He walked up the path to the lean-tos. He stepped around the fire, and the blond giant saw him. The man dropped the hide he was holding, stared at him a moment, then said to his companion, "Scanlon, we got company."

The dark one was young. He stared at Brooks, his right hand coming to rest on his hip, over the butt of his gun.

"We didn't hear no horse," the blond one said.

"I ain't got a horse." Brooks watched the hand. "You don't care much whose beef you skin," he said.

"That some business of yours?" the young one asked.

"When it's my own beef it is." As he spoke the hand moved and so did his own. He drew and fired and he saw the other twisted and staggered by his slug. The drawn gun fell unfired, and with his eyes now wide with shock and pain the dark one clutched his shoulder and began to curse him.

Brooks picked up the rifle that leaned against the tree and he walked over and picked up the fallen pistol and stuck it in his belt. He looked the two men over for a moment, then went back and entered the corral. The black horse was the best, too good for any skinner, and so, he thought, was the saddle. He slid the rifle into the saddle scabbard and tied his water bottle on, then he snapped the bit in the black's mouth and swung up, herding the other horse out of the corral before him. He gave its rump a slap with the reins so that it ran off. Then without another glance at the skinners he turned and rode off into the brush.

Chapter Eleven

At dawn, three days later, having traveled most of the way at night and holed up during the day, he returned to the hills of Tilton County, the last place, as he figured it, anyone would expect to find him now. He rode on into the hills for an hour or two, then unsaddled the black and turned him loose. He cached the saddle and set out once more to look for Willie.

For a week he climbed the hills and worked his way through the canyons, and during all that time he never heard a shot fired or caught a glimpse of another human. On the morning of the sixth day, however, he found signs of Willie. In a small clearing on a hilltop there were some ashes, some feathers from a quail and a forked stick like those Willie whittled in fashioning his snares.

He stayed in that place for an hour or more, examining the ground minutely. Then, on an outcropping of limestone he found dried blood. Was it Willie's blood, he wondered, or had it come from the quail? And why had Willie discarded that stick, once he had whittled it? He realized that for all he knew, Willie could be dead.

Though he went on searching the next day his heart was not in it. He had seen few cattle in the hills this time, and in any event he had not wanted to risk a shot. All week he had been able to snare only two small rabbits. He was hungry all the time, his feet were blistered and bleeding in his boots, and he needed a bath so bad he guessed anybody that got within a mile of him would be led right to him.

He decided to go back to the cedars where he had holed out those first few days. He had left his riata there with the saddlebags and he figured when he got the riata he would go on down to the river, rope a yearling and kill it with his knife.

It was late afternoon when he reached the cedars, and he was resting by the saddlebags when he heard a sound up above the spring and, without quite knowing what the sound had been, he was aware of a sense of danger, as if he had just heard a rattlesnake in under the cedar boughs.

After a moment, hearing nothing more, he crawled over under a tree and looked out through the dark, masking boughs toward the trail and the spring. At first he saw nothing; then, rising slowly from behind one of the knobs of limestone above the spring, the head and shoulders of a man appeared, both clothing and features blending so well with the rocks and mesquite that it was difficult to believe at first that anyone was really there. It was a moment before he could make out the face, and then it was as if he had recognized it even before he saw it. It was Matt Hunter's face, a face he had imagined so often along the lonely trails and among the trees and rocks that it did not seem surprising to him now actually to see it.

For several minutes Hunter did not move; only the eyes moved, and once Brooks felt that they looked directly into his own. Then, inch by inch, he brought the rifle to his shoulder. He felt better when he got Hunter in the sights. It's him or me, he thought. Why don't I squeeze? But he couldn't do it.

Then Hunter moved again. He rose and knelt by the fissure that contained the spring. Brooks watched him examine the surface of the rock around the fissure. Afterward he crept on moccasined feet down the rock and studied the muddy spot where the trickle of water from the spring seeped into the ground. Brooks was thankful then that he had not stopped at the spring to drink on his way to the cedars. Any sign of him that Hunter found now would be over two weeks old. Then he thought, Willie must still be alive and around, or Hunter wouldn't be here.

Presently the scout straightened. He glanced toward the cedars once more and, like a shadow in the gathering dusk, he moved down to the trail and faded away into the hills.

Brooks waited until it grew dark and the stars came out, and as he lay there in the cedars he thought of the corn in the field down at Tilton ranch. He thought of the wild plums ripe along the river, the hams and slabs of side-meat and bacon in the smokehouse. He might have waited there until dawn, because he knew he wouldn't dare build a fire at night, but he felt that unless he got something in his belly real quick he was going to be too weak to make the river at all.

The coyotes had begun to howl as he went down the trail, and after a while the blisters on his feet, that had dried while he rested, broke open again and bled; he had a dizzy spell once and found himself sitting down. When he came to the river he waded across, then laid his guns and hat on the bank and stretched out in the water in all his clothes. The September night was warm and there was a dry, hot breeze. After he got out of the water he moved cautiously along the bank, exploring the branches of the plum trees in the starlight, eating what the crows and jays had left.

The plums gave him cramps, and after he ate them his hunger became like a demon in him. He moved up into the corn patch and ravenously devoured several ears of corn; then, moving on, he saw that there was a light once more in the kitchen of the house. Just the sight of the lamplight seemed beautiful to him.

He thought of the kitchen with its scrubbed pine floor, the big black stove and the table where the lamp stood. He thought of the nights sitting at that table when the frost was on the ground and there would be a fire blazing in the stove. They would sit there, he and Mr. Tilton and Willie, and sometimes he would read selections from McGuffey out loud to Willie and Mr. Tilton, or he and Mr. Tilton would go over the tally books and the stock record books while Willie baked a Johnny cake. Then they would have some coffee and a piece of the cake before they went to bed.

Now he was aware of an irresistible curiosity to see who was there in the kitchen. Though he knew it was a crazy thing, he felt almost that if he were to go there and knock it might be Willie or Mr. Tilton himself who would open the door. And he was hungry. He was hungry, and the kitchen had always meant food.

He tried the door of the smokehouse first, but the heavy door was padlocked, just as it had always been. Carrying his boots and the rifle, he moved on toward the house. When he reached the tree in the yard he could see in the kitchen window, but he could see only the hand of the man who was sitting at the table. Whoever it was, he was reading a newspaper. Brooks watched him turn a page, then he stepped out from the tree and looked at the man's face. It was old Jules, the cook.

For a moment Brooks felt the way he had when he saw Adna Thorn, the blacksmith, riding along the trail. Jules had been a pretty good friend of his, and he found himself smiling at the sight of him; he even took an impulsive step toward the door before he checked himself.

There was a thousand dollars on Willie, probably the same amount on him. He had to remind himself that he had no friends. Only Joe Wood. Joe and Mary Silk. For a thousand dollars a rider, or a cook, would have to work three years.

After a while he forgot his hunger, forgot his loneliness. He went back down to the river and recrossed. He climbed the path to the bluffs and found a place in the brush to spend the night.

Just after dawn and a mile downriver he roped and killed a yearling. He built a small, well concealed fire, cooked some liver and ribs and ate his fill, then he washed his clothes in the river and spread them in the sun. The sight of his own image on the river's surface amazed him. Though he was aware that he had a beard and knew that his hair was long and unkempt, he hadn't realized that he looked as strange as he did; it was a wild man he saw mirrored in the river.

From his place in the brush he could see the fenced-in knoll east of the ranch house with the fresh grave on it. There were two other graves there. One belonged to Mr. Tilton's wife, who had died before Brooks was born. The other belonged to Mr. Tilton's only child, a boy who had died when he was nine years old. Brooks looked at the new grave and he wondered what Mr. Tilton would have done if he was in his place. If he could only talk to Joe, he thought. The man who killed Mr. Tilton hadn't been any trail bum. He must have been someone all of them knew. He had come from the town and returned to the town. And, sooner or later, he would start spending that gold. Joe could keep his eyes open. Joe could help him.

How could he get in touch with Joe? He thought it

over all that morning, listening to Jules as he fed the chickens and the hogs. And he thought about Jules, remembering everything he knew about him. Jules had been as friendly with him as he ever was with anyone, for the cook was subject to black, gloomy moods when he wouldn't speak to anyone at all. He had joined the gold rush to California in '49 to make his fortune. Instead, he had ended up as a cook, and he hated cooking. All he really wanted, Jules said, was a little farm in Normandy, with his own apple orchard and a nice fat wife. He would sit in the kitchen of the farm and drink calvados while his wife did all the cooking. He had saved his money many times to go back to France, but something always happened. What happened was that he had a passion for cards, and he always lost. They cheated him, he said. After one of his disastrous bouts of draw poker or seven-up you couldn't get a decent word out of him for weeks; nothing but French cusswords.

Could he approach Jules, he wondered? Could he trust him?

And then suddenly he remembered the watch.

Jules's grandfather, who had been a gamekeeper on the estate of a count, had been given the watch for saving the nobleman's life one day when a wild boar charged him. Jules wore the watch on a chain around his neck, and kept it tied up in a deerskin pouch. The watch was a delicate miracle of filigreed gold and it wound with a tiny key. Once when Jules had lost all the money he had been saving to go back to France in a game of seven-up, Brooks had asked him why he didn't sell the watch. The cook had looked at him as if he had just called his mother a bad name. The ticking of that watch was like the beating of his heart, Jules said. He would never sell it; and the man who stole it stole his life.

Once he remembered the watch, he knew he could handle Jules.

The next morning he was hidden in the corn, his rifle barrel resting on one of the pumpkins that grew among the corn. From where he lay he could look out through the stalks and see the kitchen door, the hog pen and the chicken run.

After he had been there an hour or so the kitchen door opened and Jules came out. He was wearing an undershirt and pants and one of his galluses was hanging. He was a short, heavy man with a curly gray beard and a mass of thick curly hair. He scratched himself, yawned and looked at the sky, then he heard the pigs and chickens calling for him and he started cussing them in French. He came down to the feed shed, still cussing, and got the pigs a pail of corn and a pail of sorghum. He fed the chickens and took three eggs from the hen house.

Brooks called to him as he came out of the chicken yard. "Jules—" he said, just loud enough for the cook to hear him. "I got a gun on you. Come here."

Jules stood very still for a moment, staring at the corn; then he said, "Who is it? Who are you?"

"Come here," Brooks told him grimly.

Jules came slowly to the edge of the corn patch. His dark eyes finally located Brooks and when he recognized him a wild look came over his face. "Cameron!" he said.

"Anybody else here on the place with you?" Brooks asked him.

Jules shook his head. "What do you want? You must be crazy, coming around here." He was trembling.

"Come on in here and set a while," Brooks said. "I want to talk to you, Jules."

Jules started shaking his head. "No."

"Come on," Brooks drew back the hammer of the rifle, knowing Jules could hear it. "I'm going to count," he said. "Time I count five I'll see if I can shoot them eggs out of your hand."

Jules dropped the eggs and they broke at his feet.

"One," Brooks said. When he said "Two" Jules crawled through the pole fence. He walked slowly on into the corn, peering ahead of him.

A few feet from Brooks he sat down. "Why you want to come back here?"

"I'm looking for Willie. I never killed Mr. Tilton, Jules, and neither did Willie."

Jules shrugged. "They say you did. They'll kill you just as dead if they find you, whether you did or not. You ought to get out of here, far away from here."

"I got to find Willie," Brooks said.

For a moment Jules studied his face, as if he could not understand why he said that, then he glanced down at his feet. "Willie?" he said in a slow, strange way.

"Willie saw who it was killed Mr. Tilton."

Jules shook his head. "Willie's dead."

Brooks stared at him. He heard the words but he didn't believe them. He waited until Jules met his eyes again, then he knew it was true.

"About a week ago," Jules went on, "that old man—the scout—he come by leading a horse, and Willie was on that horse. He was dead, lying slung across the saddle with his arms hanging down."

"Hunter," Brooks whispered.

"Yes," Jules said. "That one."

Brooks suddenly stared hard at an ear of corn just above Jules's head. He didn't want to think of it—Willie dead. Willie slung over a horse like the carcass of a deer, and taking with him his last hope.

Jules was watching him. "I heard they chased you to the Border. Why didn't you stay there?"

Brooks thought of Hunter rising from the rock above the spring. If Hunter had killed Willie, why had he been there? Then he knew. Somehow Hunter knew he had returned to the hills. For an instant he had the feeling Hunter could see right inside his head.

"Jules," he said abruptly. "How long since you've been to town?"

"Not since the funeral," Jules said. "Mr. Syd Tilton hired me that day to stay out here and watch the place. He was supposed to rustle up another hand, but nobody come."

"Is there a reward on me?"

"A thousand dollars."

Brooks said, watching him and still feeling the ache of Willie's death, "That's a lot of money." The cook made no reply. "I want you to go to town for me," Brooks told him then.

"Go to town for you!" Jules's eyes were round and alarmed. He started shaking his head.

Brooks stared at him a moment. Then he pulled the

hammer of the rifle back once more and the clicking sound was loud in the silence. "Jules," he said softly, "I got a hankering to see that pretty watch you wear."

"No!" Jules right hand went nervously to his throat.

"Take it off, damn it!"

"Brooks," Jules said pleadingly, "I was always your good friend."

"I got no friends," Brooks said. "Jules, take it off."

Jules fumbled with the buttons on his blue cotton shirt, then he fumbled with the catch on the watch chain. Finally he held the precious watch in his hand. "What do you want with my watch?"

"Lay it on the ground."

Jules slowly stretched out a hand, hesitated, then carefully placed the watch on the ground. Brooks leaned forward and picked it up. "Now, listen good," he said. "In the morning I want you to ride to town. You find Joe Wood and tell him private that there's a friend of his out here who would appreciate it if he'd ride out this way."

Jules shook his head. "They find out I helped you, they'll kill me too."

"If you don't do as I say you'll never see this watch again. First thing I'll do, if you go to trick me, is to put a slug through the watch."

Jules looked at the watch in its deerskin pouch. He looked at the rifle and then at Brooks. "You wasn't like this before," he said.

"Get me some socks," Brooks said. "Bring me some bread too, if you got any. And that newspaper I saw you reading."

Jules gave him two pairs of clean socks, some bread, a ham end and an old San Antonio newspaper that told of Mr. Tilton's murder and his own jailbreak.

The place he had selected as a hide-out on the bluffs lay under an outcropping of rock and was in the midst of a dense, tall growth of chaparral and mesquite. There were several trails through this thicket, but they were so narrow and overgrown that a rider, or even a man on foot, coming along one of them would be heard approaching long before he reached the small open space against the face of the rock. And, by crawling through the brush a dozen yards, Brooks could look out over the river. He could see the ranch house a mile upstream and the road that led to town.

That afternoon he lay in the shade of the rock and read the newspaper. Mr. Tilton's name was in big type; he himself was referred to as the son of the late Confederate veteran leader and firebrand, William Cameron. The paper was a Davis paper, and it carried a big editorial in black-faced type. The murder of David Tilton, the editorial said, should alert everyone to the lawless Rebel element in the electorate. If anything had been needed to insure complete victory for the Davis ticket in Tilton County, this foul murder of a revered hero of the Republic by the wild and lawless spawn of a law-defying Reb leader should do it.

He read the paper from the front page to the back page and, besides all the things it had to say about him and his dead father and the friends who had gotten him out of the jail, the news was real gloomy. There was a panic and a depression on in the country. You couldn't sell Texas beef in the eastern market at any price, because people were scared of getting tick fever from eating it. The ranches were laying off hands. San Antonio was full of out-of-work riders, and if the drought went on much longer there wouldn't be any cattle business left.

When he finished the paper he lay there and thought about Willie. Now that Willie was gone he realized how much he had been depending on him. Now he himself had to try and figure out the name he had hoped to get from Willie. He had done enough thinking about who Mr. Tilton's killer might have been to have reached the conclusion that it hadn't been any stranger that had stolen his horse from the freighters' corral and ridden out to the ranch. The killer had come from the town and had returned to the town.

In his mind he began to make a list of those who had known Mr. Tilton would be returning to the ranch alone that Saturday morning with the gold to pay the men, and the list included all the riders that had gone up the trail to Denver and back. It included Jules, just as it did the sheriff and Syd Tilton. Once he had finished the list, he began weighing each man on it in his mind, recalling all he knew about him and coming to a more or less firm conclusion as to whether he would have been capable of committing the murder or not.

When he had finished he had cut the list to five names, dropping the rest for one reason or another. Jules he dismissed, for instance, because if Jules had taken the money belt he wouldn't still be hanging around there. The same would hold true, he thought, of any of the trail riders who were still around. But he could go no further now without the help of someone in the town. He needed Joe.

It made him feel better to think it all out, to have some kind of a plan. But that night as he lay there in his hole in the brush he thought of Hunter somewhere in the hills, Hunter who had collected a thousand in gold for killing Willie, and who now must be looking for him. He thought of poor Willie hanging head-down from a horse. He thought of all the things the paper had said abut him, thought of all the risks and difficulties, the lonely days and nights of hiding ahead of him—if he lived. For a while his ever returning to Tiltonville seemed as remote and unlikely as reaching one of the stars that twinkled above him.

Chapter Twelve

At sunup next morning he was watching from the bluffs when Jules rode out from the ranch. And that afternoon, earlier than he had expected, he saw the cook come riding back.

He watched Jules unsaddle his horse in the corral. He saw him take a few steps toward the corn patch, as if he thought Brooks might be waiting there, then he slung his saddlebags over his shoulder and walked slowly up to the house. Before he entered the kitchen he turned and looked toward the hills.

Well, Brooks said to himself, as the kitchen door closed, what about it? Did Jules act right or not? He looked back along the road toward town, searching for telltale pillars of dust, but the sky above the plain shimmered hot and clear. If they were coming, he thought, they would come through the hills; they would cut him off from the south with a line of riders, flush him down across the river onto the plain.

He waited until just before dusk, then slipped down the trail to the river and crossed. From the corn patch he threw a stone that lit on the kitchen roof and in a moment Jules emerged. Jules carried a pail. He came to the edge of the corn, then he seemed to hesitate. After a moment he slipped through the fence. He picked a couple of ears of corn and dropped them into the pail. As he reached for a third ear Brooks fired. The pail went spinning—and the pistol that was in the pail had been cocked; it exploded as it hit the ground.

Jules stood trembling. He peered through the cornstalks at the rifle and Brooks could see the sweat break out on his forehead. "Come set a while," he told Jules.

Jules came in slowly and sat down. His shoulders slumped and he didn't meet Brooks's gaze. "I couldn't be sure it was you," he said. "That's why I brought the gun. I told Mr. Syd Tilton I wouldn't stay out here alone, what with all the trail bums—"

Brooks cut him short. "You knew it was me." The dusk was creeping down from the hills now and the moon was already rising, full again, coming up huge over the plain, and in its light the cook's face looked bleak and laden with guilt. "You tell Lufkin I was around here?" Brooks asked.

Jules gave a start. "No," he said after a moment. "I didn't tell him."

"What were you plannin' to do with that gun?"

"I told you. A man needs a gun with him these days."

"Try telling the truth!" Brooks snapped. "If you don't I'm goin' to keep you right with me for a while. Then if I see Lufkin or some of his people riding around out here as if they might be looking for me, I'll make sure you never live to collect any reward—let alone get your watch back."

"I wouldn't tell Lufkin and then come back out here by myself," Jules said. He gazed at Brooks and sighed. "You put a big burden on me. That thousand dollars— All the way to town I couldn't get it out of my head. What shall I do? If they find I helped you they'll hang me too. The law wants you. The right thing is that I go to the law. And, if I act right, I get a thousand dollars too. Then I get to thinking. Everybody knows how Lufkin is. If I tell him you're here, what will he do? Lufkin will come out and kill you and claim the reward himself."

"So you decided maybe you'd kill me personally."

"No—" Jules said. He shrugged wearily. "Maybe so. I don't know. What can a man do, faced with such a decision? For a while I had some drinks in the Buffalo House. I could not make up my mind. I listened to the talk. Someone was saying your friend, Joe Wood, and Lufkin, they are both courting your girl."

"What?" Brooks stared at him. He felt the blood rising and pounding in his temples.

"You told me to tell Joe you're here," Jules went on. "And I think—how does he know he can trust him. Or anybody. Suppose I tell Joe and Joe rides out and kills him. Joe collects the reward. You're dead, and I'm just an old fool who couldn't make up his mind. All the way home I thought of Normandy in the spring, with the apples blossoming. I put a gun in the pail, but I still didn't know what I would do."

Brooks said grimly, his throat dry, "Did you see Joe? Did you tell him?"

Jules nodded. "He came in the Buffalo House and I told him. But now you watch out. Syd Tilton is sending another hand out here tomorrow."

Brooks got up. "Don't worry your head over me! I'll take care of myself."

"My watch?" Jules reminded him tentatively then.

"I'll keep that watch, just to be sure you keep in line." He stared down at the cook, recognizing that his anger was not so much at him but at what he had said about Joe and Lufkin courting Mary. "Next time I see you coming toward me with a pail," he warned harshly, "it'll be you gets hit, not the pail."

Next morning he saw the dust of a rider coming along the road from town, but he could tell as soon as the man came into view that it wasn't Joe. When the rider got to the ranch he recognized him. It was an old fellow with a gimpy leg named Bill Hollis, who had worked for Mr. Tilton during the roundup that spring. Brooks watched Hollis unsaddle and go into the house with Jules.

He didn't see Joe Wood at first, because Joe came along the wash instead of the road. Joe stopped at the house and for a while he sat under the pecan tree talking to Jules and Hollis; then he got on his horse again and started along the river.

Brooks studied the wash and the plain beyond the wash and he looked back toward town. Down at the ranch Jules and Hollis remained in the saddle beneath the tree. Hollis had stretched out and he looked as if he were asleep, but Jules was smoking a cigarette and gazing off up the river after Joe.

Brooks waited a while longer; then he left the thicket and took a trail that would lead him to the river about a mile further east. He was waiting there in some brush when Joe came riding slowly along the trail on the other side of the river. There were cattle all along there, standing in the water or lying in it, and some of them were bawling their misery so loud you couldn't hear anything else. When Joe appeared beyond the cattle at the break in the trees, Brooks stood up in the brush. Joe didn't see him at first, so he took off his hat and Joe noticed the movement, looked right at him and reined in. Presently, after a glance up and down the river, he rode into the water, weaving his way through the cattle.

Brooks had sat down again and was leaning against a rock when Joe rode into the brush. "Mr. Brooks Cameron, himself!" Joe exclaimed softly. He got down and squatted, staring at Brooks. "You look like a real old brush booger."

Brooks said, "What did Jules tell you?"

"He tells me there's a friend of mine out here that would like it if I'd ride out. I just couldn't believe it could be you. Lufkin come back with a story how they chased you right into Mexico. Nobody figured ever to see you again."

"Nobody?"

Joe paid no attention to the question. "How long you been back here?"

"Week or so," Brooks said. He stared at Joe. He noticed how clean Joe looked, clean-shaven, with his jaws glistening from soap, and he had on a new hat and new boots. "What did you tell them there at the ranch?" he asked.

"Said I was looking for deer." Joe glanced at him. "You know about Willie?"

Brooks nodded. He moved his head a little so he could see out through the branches. He watched the cattle, listening. He knew that Hunter wouldn't have let out where he was going. If he had said he thought Cameron had come back to the hills everybody would be there to search again, trying to collect the reward money. Now Hunter had the hills to himself.

Joe said, "Why do you want to come back and hang around here? I don't figure that."

"I'm going to find the man that killed Mr. Tilton," Brooks said.

Joe snapped the twig he was fooling with and stared at him. "Everybody thinks now it was you," he said after a moment. "Even some that didn't at first."

"The man that killed Mr. Tilton got that money belt," Brooks said. "The man that killed him went back to town. He's somebody you know, and he ain't me." He told Joe how he had been thinking over the ones who might have done it, and he named the five men left on his list, counting the names off on his fingers. Tarrant Smith was one, and there were two other riders who had gone on the trail with them, Faber and Collins. Then there were Lufkin and Syd Tilton.

"Syd Tilton?" Joe said in a surprised way.

"He gets all the Tilton money now, doesn't he? Anyhow, either Syd or Lufkin might have figured I'd get blamed for it. Or, if it didn't work out that way, there was always Willie to blame—or the first rider to come out to the ranch for his pay. You were all sore at Mr. Tilton."

Joe shook his head. "How you think you're going to prove anything—even if you should find out who it was?"

"Whoever killed Mr. Tilton is wearing that money belt right now. Or they got it hid."

"That doesn't mean they're still around here with it."

"Wait a minute," Brooks told him. "Let's start with Tarrant Smith. Is he still around?"

"Tarrant's out at his brother's place."

"Did he collect his pay?"

Joe nodded. "Syd Tilton paid us. We had to wait three days."

"Did all the other riders collect their pay?"

Joe laughed. "You think anybody'd ride off without it?"

Brooks nodded. "The one with that money belt would have. If it was Collins or Faber, they wouldn't have headed back to town. They ain't from around here. If one of them killed Mr. Tilton he would have already had his pay, plus everybody else's."

Joe pushed back his hat and ran his fingers through his hair. "I don't know if everybody collected pay or not. I know Tarrant did. He went with me."

"Were Collins and Faber around town after Sunday?"

Joe regarded him blankly for a moment as he tried to think back, then he shook his head. "I don't remember. I moved out of the freighter bunkhouse over to my aunt's house that Sunday."

"Can you go to Syd Tilton to see if they got their pay? You could tell him you want to look at the wage book— you figure there was some mistake. Then you could check all the names."

Joe nodded reluctantly. "Sure. I guess I could," he said. "If Faber and Collins collected pay, that will rule them out. That will leave just Tarrant, Lufkin and Syd Tilton."

Joe gazed at him. "How about me?"

Brooks said, "It ain't exactly your style. For another thing, you couldn't have hold of all that money, even for a day, without wanting to spend it. And you're not a big enough damn fool to think you could spend it around Tiltonville. If it was you, you'd be someplace else." He gazed back at Joe steadily. "Unless of course there was some special reason that was causing you to hang around Tiltonville."

"If it was Lufkin or Syd," Joe said, "they never would spend that money. Syd would just put it in his safe."

"And to make things look good he'd figure he could afford to offer a couple of thousand dollars in rewards," Brooks said.

"If it was Lufkin," Joe went on, "he'd have that gold hid. He'd throw his own mother in jail for a dollar, and then he'd never part with the dollar, either."

"Tarrant would have it hid, too."

"Yeah," Joe agreed. "Tarrant is smart and foxy. He'd hide that belt and he'd wait till everything died down. Then one day he'd dig it up and ride out of Tiltonville for good."

"How would Lufkin figure to use that money?" Brooks wondered.

Joe gave him an odd look. "Maybe he'd figure to get married with it," he said.

"Married to who?"

"Brooks," Joe said, "you know he's courting Mary."

Brooks said, "She wouldn't have nothin' to do with Lufkin."

Joe shook his head. "You don't know how it is. You got to figure you might just as well be dead, as far as Mary or Tiltonville is concerned. You can't ever go back there."

"I am going back."

"Brooks," Joe said softly, "you got to face it. You ain't got a chance in a million. Oh, sure—it's fine talkin' and figurin' who might be the guilty party. But it's just crazy, you hidin' out here in the brush, thinkin' you can find that party, prove it on him, and square everything for yourself. I'm your friend, and I'm tellin' you. Git, boy. Light out. Do it while you're still livin' to do it."

Brooks said, "Go on—tell me. What about Mary and Lufkin?"

Joe said, "Her folks like him. The reverend takes to him because he doesn't smoke or drink. Everybody else knows he doesn't smoke or drink just because he's too close to spend the money. But the reverend doesn't know that. Like I say—it's not as if you were still around, or ever would be again."

"You tryin' to tell me she likes Lufkin?"

"No," Joe said. "She doesn't. But her folks are drivin' her crazy, pushin' her at him. He's there every night, settin' in the parlor with her and them, talkin' about himself. He's asked the reverend for her hand and the reverend has said yes."

Brooks said grimly, "I got to see her."

"Don't talk crazy, boy!"

"You tell her I'll meet her tomorrow night. You hear? She knows the place."

"You can't ride in there," Joe said.

"I can; I'm going to!"

"What good would it do, seein' her? What good would it do either of you?"

"Joe—" Brooks said. He stared at him. "I asked you to tell her."

Joe didn't answer for a while, then he said, "That why you sent for me, is it?"

"No," Brooks told him. "I figured you could check to see who got paid. I figured you might look and see if Tarrant or Lufkin had let their belts out a couple of notches from wearin' a money belt under their shirts."

Joe shook his head. "What good will it do?"

Brooks didn't answer that. He didn't say anything for a moment, then he asked suddenly, "Tell me, Joe—have you been courtin' Mary too?" He watched Joe's skin redden beneath the tan, and Joe did not look at him. For a moment he stared over at his horse. Down on the river the cattle bawled and there were small sounds of birds hopping in the brush.

"You want to see her forced into marryin' Lufkin?"

"You have been seeing her then?"

"I been seein' her when I can. It ain't as if you was there, as if I was cuttin' in on you. It ain't as if you was ever likely to be able to marry her." He shrugged. "I'm no prize, but the way I figure, it would be better if she married me than Lufkin."

Brooks was silent for a long time. Finally he said, "You going to tell her for me about tomorrow night?"

Joe got to his feet. "If that's the way you want it," he said slowly, "I'll tell her." He swung up on his horse and looked down at Brooks. "So long," he said.

"So long," Brooks told him.

Brooks sat there for a while after Joe left, then he got up and started back toward his thicket, and the way he felt he thought he might just as well crawl in there and die.

He thought of what Joe had said, and it seemed true about his ever finding the killer of Mr. Tilton and proving it on him. He didn't have a chance. And it seemed true what Joe had said about Mary and him. What right did he have to see her? What did he have to offer her? Yes, it was true—as far as Tiltonville and Mary were concerned he might as well be dead. But as he came into the little clearing that was his hide-out he said to himself: Anyhow, I won't give up. I won't run. One way or another, I'm going to keep trying.

"Sure now," a voice drawled from the thicket. "Drop your guns, Cameron!"

He dropped the rifle and whirled, drawing and firing at the same instant, firing blindly into the rocks and brush. And, even as he pulled the trigger, he was waiting for the crash of Matt Hunter's buffalo gun—knowing it would be the last sound he would ever hear.

Chapter Thirteen

As Brooks pulled the trigger he had moved toward
the shelter of some rocks, then lunged for their cover. Now,
as the roar of his firing echoed away, he was surprised to
find himself lying behind the rocks, still alive and unhurt.
He was just wondering if by some miracle he had managed
to hit Hunter with one of his shots, when he heard his
voice again.

"Cameron," Hunter said, "toss that gun away and we'll
talk."

Brooks moved his head, trying to guess where Hunter
was. He knew the scout must have changed position in the
brush while he was firing at him.

"I could kill you right now," Hunter said. "I got a bead
on you this minute."

It was probably true, Brooks realized. If Hunter had been
going to kill him he could easily have done it when he
entered the clearing. "I'll talk," he agreed, finally, "but I'm
hanging onto my gun."

"All right," Hunter said. "Holster it."

He hesitated, then slid the gun into its holster and rolled
over. He sat up, his back against the rocks, his hand still
on the gun butt. From the thicket a rifle barrel emerged,
above it Hunter's face.

"You're mighty fast and fancy with that gun," Hunter
said. "But don't be. Forget it now, I tell you, or I'll blow
the lights out of you and get paid gold money for my
trouble."

Brooks gazed at him, feeling the fire of his hatred burning in his eyes. To him Hunter was an apparition, a weird
and ghostly figure from some earlier time, as well as his
own personal haunt, the Willie-killer, the shadow that
stalked him through the hills and saw inside his head. In
the gloom of the thicket the old scarecrow in buckskin was
not real; only the buffalo gun he held was real, the big .50
that had left the cities of buffalo bones on the northern
plains.

Hunter moved out of the thicket and sat upon a stone, relaxed, yet wary as a snake. "I been watchin' you two days now," he said. "I had you in my sights a couple of times. I killed your breed friend, and I figure you just found that out. So you won't wait around here no longer. I tell you I killed him, even if I didn't go to kill him. The worst I figured he'd get from my ball is a busted leg, but just as I squeezed her off he moved and I caught him fair. I figured to talk to that breed. I was thinkin' if he didn't have somethin' on him I might hear from him where it was."

Brooks gazed steadily into the pale eyes. Hunter grinned, showing blackened stubs of teeth. He brought his left hand up carefully, still holding the rifle with his right, his finger curled around the trigger, the muzzle pointing steadily at Brooks. He pulled a few shreds of tobacco from a pocket of his greasy shirt and popped them in his mouth, then he slowly flexed his left arm.

"You nicked me good that day over to the west," he said. "She still aches on me." He grinned again and spat a stream of tobacco juice at Brooks's feet. "I ought to be riled at you, but I ain't. You got her on you now, ain't you? If you got her, hand her over and we'll be all square."

He meant the money belt, Brooks thought. Hunter hadn't intended to kill Willie because if Willie didn't have the money belt on him he had figured he could find out where it was.

"That sidekick of yours rode out here today," Hunter went on. "He told you I killed the breed. You was looking for that breed friend, but you couldn't find him. Then you was goin' to wait a while for him to show up here. Now you got no good reason to wait." He grinned once more and spat, this time hitting Brooks's boots. "Where is she, boy? You got her on you?"

There was a silence while Hunter waited for him to speak, and after a while he nodded just as if Brooks really had said something, then he went on talking, as if to say he was a patient man, and anyhow they had all the time in the world and, if Brooks didn't want to talk any, what could be more pleasant to listen to than the sound of his own voice.

He said, "I stalked that breed. I seen his sign. I knowed

the part he was around and I staked myself out on a hill-top, laying three days in the brush. The third day he showed himself in a little clearin' over on the next hill and, like I say, I didn't go to kill him. I aimed to hit him in the leg, but just as I squeezed her off he bent over for some-thing. Then when I get to where he is he's lyin' there on his back breathin' blood and lookin' up at me, his front all bloody, and I know he ain't got long."

Brooks stared at the face before him and thought of Willie, Willie who wouldn't hurt anybody, Willie lying there like Hunter said. His fingers tightened on the gun butt and he thought it would be good to draw the gun and make a hole between the pale eyes that watched him so intently now. He knew he could draw and do it just at the same instant the buffalo gun would be blasting him out of the world. He knew he could do it, and Hunter knew he could do it.

Hunter waited a moment, then went on. "So I hunkered down there by him," he said. "I felt for that money belt, but he don't have her on. 'Who's got that belt?' I asked him. 'Cameron got it?'" Hunter shook his head. "He don't answer me. He just crosses himself. 'You kill old man Tilton?' I asked him. 'You kill him, or was it Cameron done it?' Well, sir, he just crosses himself again. Then he closes them eyes of his and quit breathing."

Willie, Brooks thought—crossed himself? It didn't make sense to him.

Hunter continued, "I didn't learn me much from that breed. But I saw your sign in the hills again." He cackled and spat again, hitting the toe of Brooks's right boot. "That boot of yours. Them big rawhide stitches where she's mended make you easy to track as a three-toed cougar. I was there at sunup the next mornin' to that place you jumped us over in the western hills. I seen that boot track, and I seen it again over here while I was huntin' the breed. I knowed you was around here, but nobody else did and I got to figurin', and I figured there was a good chance you might come moseyin' back."

Brooks stared at him. The hand on the gun butt had be-gun to sweat.

"First place," Hunter went on, "that money belt was

hid before you went sallyin' into town that day thinkin' you was goin' to get away with killin' the old man. Then I killed that breed and he ain't got the belt. If you didn't have it on you when they jumped you then I figure you'll be back for it." He patted his middle. "I been totin' a thousand in gold around, and that much is heavy enough. I figure you ain't been traipsin' up and down the hills lookin' for your friend with three times that amount stropped around you."

"You figure!" Brooks said. "Go on, old man—keep right on figuring." Brooks watched the pale eyes glow in the pale gray light.

"I'm figurin'," Hunter said. "I'm figurin' you got her on you or you got her hid. And now you know your breed friend is dead you think you'll dig her up and git. Or maybe the breed hid the belt, and you don't know where!" Hunter's eyes were fastened intently on his face. "Maybe that's why you been so bound to find him."

"Keep figuring."

Hunter said nothing for a moment, and when he went on it was in his old cunning, self-satisfied drawl. "Oh, it ain't I hanker for the money," he said. "I got enough gold now to keep me sinnin' the rest of my days." He cackled. "It's just a plain good time for me to follow you around. Was I to kill you, the fun would be over. And was I to kill you and find you ain't got that belt on you, why I'd be plumb miserable forever afterward wonderin' where it was." He gazed at Brooks a moment longer; then, like a snake uncoiling, he rose.

"Just don't never figure to outsmart old Matt Hunter," he said. "Don't you do it." Then he laughed that dry, cackling laugh of his again that sounded like a rattlesnake's warning, and he put one moccasined foot behind him and melted into the brush.

Before the moon rose Brooks left the thicket. He made his way down to the river and crossed, and he had no illusions. He knew Hunter would have heard him and would be following him. He walked along the river bank until he came to the pole fence around the fragrant night mass of corn. He crawled through the fence and moved deep into the corn and just as the moon rose he lay down there, on the dry, sweet-smelling earth.

Hunter, he thought, wouldn't be sure now just where he was. The old man would circle up toward the corral. He would wait. Perhaps, he would guess, finally, where he must be, and he would puzzle over that. Perhaps he would figure the money belt was hidden in the corn. But, whether Brooks now had the money belt or not, he would guess that Brooks's next move would be to take a horse from the corral. And when he had thought things through that far Brooks decided that Hunter would probably go back and get his own horse, wherever he had left it, then he would wait and see what happened. Hunter wouldn't want the men on the ranch to know he was in the vicinity; he wouldn't want to show himself any more than Brooks did.

To think of Hunter out there ghosting around in the moonlight chilled his blood—a man who wouldn't take a chance on killing him and getting only the reward money when he might get the reward and Mr. Tilton's belt full of gold too. Lying there, he began to think of the money belt. Suppose he had killed Mr. Tilton and taken the belt, then had ridden back to town. As Hunter said, he wouldn't have worn that belt to town; he would have hidden it on the way.

Again, as he had so often during the lonely nights in the brush, he tried to reconstruct that fateful morning of Mr. Tilton's death. He saw Mr. Tilton shaving at the bench outside the kitchen door. He saw a faceless, nameless rider approaching along the wash, riding Brooks's own horse, Star. He saw Willie down at the river, catching Mr. Tilton's perch.

The rider had been someone Mr. Tilton knew. The old man hadn't taken his gun from the holster of the gunbelt that hung from the peg on the kitchen wall. He had even taken a couple of steps toward the rider, maybe asking him why he was riding Brooks's horse. Then the rider had drawn and fired, shot Mr. Tilton down as he stood there with his face only half shaved. And it had been someone who knew Willie, who knew how Willie would react.

He saw Willie coming up from the river, Willie who had heard the shot, seen the killer, and fled.

Then he saw himself riding out toward the ranch, the stale, raw memory of the Buffalo House whisky in his mouth, the ache in his head, the ache in his heart for the things he had said to Mr. Tilton, things that were true but shouldn't have been said. He heard the shot echoing over the plain and later saw Willie riding up the bluffs. At that time the killer would have been spurring back along the wash, riding a horse to death, and he wouldn't have stopped to hide the money belt then. But when he came to the place where he had tied his own horse in the wash—when he stopped there to change horses—he might have hidden the belt; then, leisurely, on his own unlathered horse, he could have ridden back into town.

Chapter Fourteen

HE SLEPT IN THE CORNFIELD that night, and the constant, melancholy bawling of the cattle was an accompaniment to his dreams. He would sleep, only to wake all at once with every sense alert. Then he would fall into a dream again; he would see Hunter, pale-eyed, drifting through the corn. He would dream of Mary, and when the dawn came he felt that if he could only live through that day, if he could just endure until he saw her in the evening, until he touched her, heard her sweet voice whisper his name once more, then nothing else that could happen to him would matter much.

The morning dragged while he lay on his back and watched the birds hopping among the pumpkins beneath the corn. He watched the changes in the green-filtered light as the sun inched higher. He heard Jules feed the pigs and chickens and, when the cattle stopped their bawling for a moment, he could hear the river murmuring over the sandbars. Toward noon he ate his last bit of dry beef, chewing methodically on the stringy fibers; then he took a swig from his water bottle and went to sleep again, dozing and waking all through the afternoon.

At dusk he started crawling toward the edge of the corn. As the last light faded he lay near the fence and studied the four horses in the corral. There was a sure-footed bay from the remuda in there now, and he knew that was the one he would ride. At dark he crawled out to the fence and made his way up to the corral.

The horses knew him, and there was no dog to bark, for after the death of Mr. Tilton's old hound he'd sworn he'd never have another. In the harness shed he felt for a saddle, a bridle and blanket, as he had done in the darkness often before. Then he had to get a rope and rope the bay and tie her up short while he put a saddle on her back.

When he had the saddle on he took the gate poles down and let the other horses out. He knew they would run downriver where the rest of the remuda was grazing in the mesquite brakes, and he knew that Hunter, somewhere out there in the blackness, would probably follow them. He waited a while, then rode out. He crossed the creek, and holding the bay to a walk, went on up to the wash and turned toward town.

Two hours later, in the light of the moon, he rode out onto the San Antonio road. He rode south along the road, and when he came to the junction of the western road he could look up it and see the lights glowing on the main street of the town. He could see figures moving in front of the hotel, the dark bulk of the courthouse, the jail. And to be there again gave him an odd feeling—it was as if he had come back in one of his dreams.

At the place where the stages forded he crossed the river and turned west, following the trail along the bank of the river until he came to a clump of willows, where he dismounted and tied the horse. There were cattle moving all along the river there, and the old cottonwoods across the river masked the moon. He walked out onto a sandbar, jumped to another, then waded a shallow channel and came among the trees, smelling them again, remembering them again on that June night with Mary.

With the light drifting down through the leaves he made his way into the grove until he came to the rock that he remembered and that she would remember, and he sat down there to wait for her. He was aware of his heart pounding against his ribs, aware of the tight, dry feeling in his throat.

Would she come? Now that he was actually there he couldn't quite believe in it.

Then, almost at once, he heard careful steps on the path. Someone was moving down the path toward him and in a moment he heard the sound of tuneless humming. A voice said, "I'm Joe," then began humming again. Abreast of the rock a figure paused.

"Joe—" Brooks said. His only thought was that she had not come.

"Yeah. It's me." Joe moved toward him and sat down on the rock. "Mary's got to wait till Lufkin leaves," he said. "Then she's got to wait till her folks get to sleep before she can slip out."

Brooks said nothing. He swallowed, for his throat was like dust again. She was coming to him.

"Lufkin," Joe went on softly, "ordered him a little ring in the mail from San Antone, little old thing with a diamond in it that it takes a good pair of specs to see. Now he's trying to get Mary to put that ring on her finger, and her folks are trying to get her to do it too."

Joe sounded tense. "Brooks," he said, "something's got to be done, and we're goin' to do it. I talked to Mary right after sundown. We got plans for us."

"Plans?" Brooks said slowly. "What plans?" He thought of Lufkin with the ring, trying to put it on Mary's finger.

Joe whispered, "We're goin' to California, Brooks."

Brooks turned his head and stared at the dark outline of Joe's face. "Who is?" he asked, finally.

"Mary and me," Joe said. "And you. I'll take her out there and we'll meet you." Joe waited for him to say something, then went on. "She can't stay here in Tiltonville with her folks—not the way things are. And she's got no other kin. She's either got to run off, or marry Lufkin, or marry somebody else."

"California—" Brooks said slowly.

"She figures she could be with you there. Nobody way out there's likely to have heard of you, or even Mr. Tilton. I been talkin' to some freighters who was there; they say it's mighty pretty, and cattle country too. I figure you and me could go in the cattle business there. They're makin' up trail herds now, the freighters said, west of the Pecos and in New Mexico, to drive there. There's a good beef market out there, they said."

"Mary—" Brooks said. "She wants to go?"

"Anywhere she can get together with you. And she's scared to have you hanging around. Then, like I been tellin' you, there's Lufkin—"

"How would you take her?"

"I'd get me a rig. She'd slip out one night and we'd drive all night to the pass. We'd catch the western stage there in the mornin', when they stop to change horses. I figure you could get to the Pecos and join up with one of them trail outfits. Then we'd meet you in California. There's a hotel in Los Angeles these freighters give me the name of—the Mission Hotel. A big place, right on the plaza there. You can't miss it, they said." Joe stopped. "How does it sound to you?"

"I dunno," Brooks said after a moment.

"You dunno!" Joe exclaimed softly. "What do you want to do—just hide out here in the brush till somebody catches sight of you and puts a bullet in you? What about Mary? What's she goin' to do? You want Lufkin to put that ring of his on her?"

"I've got to think about it," Brooks said. "I'll talk to Mary."

After a moment Joe got up. "Well," he said, "you think on it. You talk to Mary." He waited a moment. "So long."

"Joe," Brooks said, "did you see Syd Tilton? Did you get a look at that wage book?"

"I did," Joe said, "Everybody got paid. Everybody but you."

"Nobody spending money around?"

"Nobody got it to spend. Not even Lufkin. Brooks—you got to give it up, settin' out there in the brush, figurin' yourself crazy over who it was."

"Lufkin wouldn't spend it—not even if he had it."

"Sure. On Mary he would. Who wouldn't spend it on her?"

Brooks thought about her, and now that was all he could think of. His heart had started pounding again and he scarcely noticed when Joe left. He thought of Lufkin there in the Reverend Silk's parlor. He saw the ring in Lufkin's fat hands. Lufkin trying to marry her! The idea sickened and enraged him.

When she finally came along the path, a beam of moonlight struck her hair, illuminated her face so that it appeared to float toward him through the trees. She hesitated, then saw him rise from the rock. She came right into his arms. She was crying as he kissed her, clinging to him, whispering his name over and over when she could, her soft cool hands touching his cheeks, pushing back his hat, in his hair.

101

"Oh, Brooks—" she whispered. "Every day I died a little."

Brooks said, "I been fine." He stroked her hair. "What's all this about Lufkin?"

"Didn't Joe tell you?"

"Yes," he said.

"He told you about California? He told you how we plan?"

"To go there?"

"Yes. Then you'd be safe, not forever running or hiding, with everybody out to kill you. Away out there—nobody'd know us. We could be together—man and wife."

He was silent for a time, and then he said, "You want me to go? You want me to run away?"

Her voice was taut, passionate. "I don't want you killed! I don't want to watch them bringing you in on a horse."

"Then everyone would always think I did it," he said. "They'd be sure that I killed Mr. Tilton."

"What difference does it make what they'd think?" She clutched him. "We'd be together. That's the only important thing there is in this world to me. It's only the hope of our being together that makes me go on living. You think I'd marry Lufkin—let anybody else ever touch me but you? I'd kill myself before I would!"

"Your pa—" he said. "He's down on me?"

"Since you broke jail. He couldn't understand you'd never get a fair trial, or that they wanted to lynch you. Since then he won't hear your name mentioned. Oh, Brooks," she whispered, "don't break my heart. I can't go on worrying over you. I can't stay on here with them thrusting Lufkin at me. Oh, Brooks—please come to California."

He thought about it, and after a while he said, "It's going to cost some, on the stage. Where'll you get the money for it?"

"I have a little," she said. "And Joe—he's got money saved."

"Joe?" he said.

"You can get to Santa Fe easily," she went on. "Like Joe says—all you got to do is ride up the Red and throw in with some freighters heading west along the trail. We can meet you in Santa Fe at the stage station, and go on together from there."

"In Santa Fe," he repeated slowly, "at the stage station." He waited a moment. "When would you leave?"

"We could leave in a night or two. Soon as you say you will." She held him close. "Brooks, you got to."

"Just give me a couple more days."

"Why?"

"There's something I want to do."

"When will I see you?"

"I'll meet you here night after tomorrow," he said.

He was kissing her again when he heard the voices. He opened his eyes, saw the lanterns and sprang up, pulling her to her feet. There were horses coming down the path. Then they both heard the Reverend Ben Silk's pulpit baritone. "Adam," he said, "I just can't believe it."

The answering voice belonged to Adam Lufkin, but Brooks couldn't make out what he said. He took Mary's arm and hurried her back through the trees and when the horses were past he whispered to her, "Run! Get back to your room."

"Brooks—" She flung her arms around his neck and kissed him and then she left.

He waited for a moment after she had gone, watching the lanterns bobbing along the path. He thought the horses would keep on along the river, but suddenly they turned and started coming back. He made a break for the river then, but just as he was wading the channel between the bars the moon sailed free of a tree mass across the river and caught him with a pale pencil of light. He heard a shout back on the path and he lunged up onto the far sandbar and ran.

"Stop!" Reverend Silk roared.

"We know who you are!" Lufkin called.

As he leaped for the saddle of the bay, the horses were entering the river. And as the bay sprang from the brush he heard them floundering over the sandbars.

The bay hit the trail running hard. But even as he leaned forward along the bay's neck, urging him on with knees and reins, his impulse was to pull in, to wheel the horse and come face to face with Lufkin. He was sick of running, sick of waiting and hiding.

Then the Reverend Silk's voice welled up behind him again, rolled on past him. "Stop, I say! We've seen you, Joe Wood!"

Joe! Brooks thought. They think it's Joe! He turned the horse into the fording.

In the water and crossing the rocks the bay did not break stride. And now, the moon behind him, he let the bay run on the north road and did not pull him until he was a mile or more beyond the turnoff for the Tilton ranch. The night was black, and there was no sound along the road. After letting the bay horse blow, he rode him east onto the plain, circling gradually toward the wash.

Joe had said Los Angeles. She had said Santa Fe. He thought about that as he rode. He thought about his friend Joe. Someone must have seen Joe going down toward the river; then someone must have seen Mary. Either that, or her parents had discovered she was not in her room.

North of the wash that paralleled the Tilton ranch road there were stands of mesquite, of densely growing brush that in places ran down into the wash. Into that rocky channel, when the rains came, the water would pour from the northern plain and after several days of rain it would become a foaming torrent.

After a few miles he came to the wash and rode down into it. He unsaddled, tethered the bay in the mesquite and lay down on the saddle blanket. He thought of California, tried in his mind to make that far place real, to see himself there with Mary, but he couldn't do it. He had known from the first he wouldn't go—no matter what. He was part of the rocks and mesquite he lay among; he belonged under these stars.

Chapter Fifteen

With the first light Brooks was up. He tied the bay horse in a thicket where nobody, even if they came along the wash, would see it. Then he started walking up the wash until he came to the skeleton of his grulla horse.

Now he tried to put himself in the killer's place. He could see the rider springing from the staggering gray with Mr. Tilton's money belt heavy in his hand. Nearby was the oak tree where the killer's own horse had been tied. If he were the killer, Brooks thought, this is where he would have hidden the belt before he rode on into town.

The wash was wide there, and perhaps twenty feet below the level of the plain. There were thickets of mesquite and many rocks, the banks being a tumbled confusion of boulders, brush and shade, while the trail wound among miniature pinnacles and buttresses of eroded limestone.

Standing by the skeleton of his horse he decided to use the skeleton as a hub and work out from it in expanding circles. He began to search at once, turning over a pile of nearby stones, then moving on to the next likely spot within the scope of his first circle.

The sun climbed as his circles widened; he cut his hands on the rocks and he was already unbearably thirsty, for he had left his water bottle in the cornfield. Occasionally he would stop and sit in the shade for a while and think again of California and Mary. He would stare thoughtfully at the rocks, the places left yet to look, and he would wonder if he weren't mad, the way he had things figured. He would wonder if maybe hiding out so long and being alone so much hadn't got him touched in the head. He would think of Joe again, Joe telling him to ride west, while Mary said ride up to the Santa Fe trail.

Then he would think of Hunter. He would stop breathing and listen. He would glance up at the banks of the wash, and stare back along the trail.

By noontime he felt he had exhausted every possible hiding place in that area. His thirst had increased to the point where it didn't seem to him he could wait for the comparative safety of nightfall to ride down to the river. One reason he continued looking among the rocks was because he was less aware of his thirst while he was working than when he sat in the shade and thought about it.

By mid-afternoon he had carefully searched an area that extended at least fifty yards along the trail in either direction from the skeleton of the horse. He had just seen one snake and when he moved the stone and saw the skin he thought at first it was another, and his instinct was to drop the stone and jump back. Then, as an exact image of what he had seen in the small crypt between the stones registered in his brain, he sank to his knees and stared. He was, he realized, looking at a money belt. After a moment he reached for it.

Inscribed on the inner surface of the belt in black, spidery pen strokes was: David Tilton, Tilton County, Texas. He opened a pocket of the belt and saw the gold eagles inside.

He jumped up with a shout of triumph welling in his throat—and something hit him, a crash of sound rolled over the wash and he was lying flat on his back among the stones, the breath knocked out of him, feeling that something had just torn away his entire left side.

He lay perfectly still and as the numbness left he could feel blood gushing, and the pain was like a burning iron. He lay, scarcely breathing, his eyes almost shut, with the sun on his face. After the crash of the buffalo gun the silence was intense. The silence was a thread upon which he dangled, his life running out while he waited for some sound, some sign.

At last the small noise of a stone falling tolled like a bell in his ears. There was a flicker of movement in a thicket above the north bank of the wash. The sun caught the dull, blued outline of a rifle barrel, and when he saw the barrel move, centering on him, he drew and fired. He fired twice, and the buffalo gun bellowed again too, kicking up rock fragments that stung his face. He rolled then into the shelter of a boulder, sat erect and quickly began tearing pieces from his shirt, stuffing and packing the gushing hole in his side.

He knew he had hit Hunter. He was certain of it as he sat there, giddy with pain and loss of blood, but he also felt sure he had not killed Hunter. And now the outline of the time ahead became clear. Either he or Hunter might leave that place, but it would only be one of them.

When he had checked the bleeding of the wound he lay prone again, inching along the face of the boulder until he found a narrow aperture formed by the boulder and another rock through which he could see the thicket where Hunter was, or where he had been. Now there was only one way for Hunter to move, and that was up the wash, where he would still have the cover of the thicket. Despite the utter stillness of the blazing afternoon, he knew he would probably hear or see nothing when the scout did move. If Hunter, unobserved, could get far enough up the wash and then cross it or come down along it, Hunter would have him at his mercy.

As he was thinking of this he heard a tiny click over in the thicket. Then it was almost as if he were over there; he could see the pale, slitted eyes of the scout, could visualize him, now that he had attended to his own wound, grimly reloading—for the clicking sound had been made by a breech bolt.

He needed to make only one mistake now, and that would be the end of it. He had to anticipate exactly what Hunter would do. As he had already decided, Hunter, keeping to the cover of the thicket, would probably make his way up the wash. But he could, of course, stay just where he was.

Now, stretched out in the full glare of the sun, and with the sudden dehydration due to his wound, his thirst was raging. His lips were puffed and dry and his tongue felt as if it were crusted with alkali dust. Still, in his intense effort to use his eyes and ears, he tried to forget his thirst. He lay, taking long, measured breaths, staring steadily across the glare of rocks toward the thicket.

Finally, as the minutes dragged on, there was movement. About fifteen yards west of the point where Hunter had been, a small bird suddenly flew up from the thicket, hovered a moment in the air, then swooped down into the wash to light on a rock.

He watched the bird. He listened to the small sounds it was making. In a few minutes the bird flew back over the thicket, circled, and then settled in the same spot it had left. So, he thought, Hunter must have passed that point. And if he believed that, it was time for him to start moving. In doing so he had no desire to test his interpretation of the bird's behavior by exposing himself.

He stopped watching the thicket and began to study the prospect of rocks and brush behind him. What he wanted was a position that would be advantageous whether Hunter came down along the wash itself or crossed to the other bank; also one that would serve him if Hunter had remained where he was. These considerations simplified and restricted his sphere of movement to just one route. This route lay on an oblique from the boulder to the south bank of the wash, where an eroded crevice cut into the soil of the plain above, and all along, among the rocks and brush, there was adequate cover.

As soon as he had each move figured out he started crawling, and when he did he could feel the wound begin to throb and bleed again, the blood seeping through the rags from his shirt and dripping onto the stones. Keeping the boulder he had left between himself and the thicket, he made his way to the next group of rocks, rested there for a moment and went on. The stones he crawled over cut his knees and hands and, though the distance from the boulder to the crevice that was his objective was not more than thirty yards, he felt it was taking him forever, that he might reach the bank only to find himself staring for one last instant up into the muzzle of the buffalo gun.

When he had crawled about two thirds of the way he reached a place he had been unable to see and anticipate from the boulder. Here for a distance of several yards, although he would be shielded from the thicket and the bank ahead, he would be in full view of Hunter, if Hunter were now somewhere up the wash.

He waited for a while, listening, and the afternoon stillness was just as intense as before. Then he drew his gun, cocked it, and started across the opening between the rocks. He was almost to the shelter of the rocks beyond when up the wash he saw Hunter dragging himself across the trail.

One leg of Hunter's buckskins was slashed open and he had a bloody bandanna tied around his thigh. He wasn't looking at Brooks; he was looking back in the direction of the boulder. But as Brooks lifted the gun Hunter saw him. Brooks fired, too quickly at that range, and Hunter had his rifle to his shoulder just as Brooks fired a second shot. Then Brooks felt his head ringing as if a hornet had just stung him above the right ear, and while the buffalo slug went shrieking and ricocheting among the rocks behind him, and the roar of the big gun slammed along the wash, he glimpsed Hunter stagger, clutch his chest and lurch into the sheltering brush beside the trail. He got off another shot then, sending a slug into the brush where the scout had vanished, and after that he scrambled up among the rocks ahead and flung himself there, panting and dizzy.

He ejected the empty cartridges from the cylinder of the gun and reloaded it. The blood from the bullet crease above his ear was running down his cheek into his beard, and the hole in his side was on fire. After he had rested for a moment he struggled out of his tattered shirt, tore it some more and made a new packing for the wound. He used strips from the shirt to bind the packing, then he stretched out on his back, exhausted, and presently from up the wash he heard the sound of Hunter's coughing.

The sun had sunk behind the hills by the time he crawled up into the crevice, and though he had not heard Hunter coughing again he did not allow himself to believe that he might be dead. He felt Hunter would take a lot more killing. Nor would he permit himself the thought that he might be the one who would die there. From the crevice he could see the coiled fat shape of the money belt lying in the wash beside the boulder. If he died, the presence of the money belt would be the final, damning evidence that he had killed Mr. Tilton.

With the passing of the sun a soft, mauve shadow fell upon the plain. He felt stronger, and his thirst oppressed him less. His one resolve now was that it would be Hunter who should die, not himself; and after a while he left the crevice and began crawling through the scanty brush that grew along that bank of the wash.

When he came abreast of the place where he had seen

Hunter vanish, he lay for a time and listened. Then he picked up a small stone and flung it down into the wash. After the stone fell he heard nothing, and he had just picked up another stone and raised himself to throw it when the buffalo gun roared behind him and his hat was slammed forward over his eyes.

For a moment he was too stunned to do anything but hug the ground, taking advantage of the slight depression in which he lay. And in front of him now he could see his hat, the crown ripped and scorched by the .50-caliber slug which, had it been an inch lower, would have been final for him. It was clear that Hunter, despite his wounds, was at least as active as himself. While he was crawling along the bank of the wash, Hunter must have been working his way down the wash and had crept up out of it somewhere behind him, perhaps just in time to see him as he lifted himself to throw the second stone.

Now he could see no possible advantage in remaining where he was. There was only one thing he could do, and that was to go back down into the wash again, try to cross it undetected, and gain the thicket on the far side. From there he would be in a commanding position if Hunter re-entered the wash. But even as he started inching down the shallow gully into the wash, he realized that the light was fading. The shadow that covered the plain had grown somber, the shapes of the rocks seemed to change and the brush across the way had taken on the purplish hues of an autumn twilight.

As he wormed his way down through the mesquite he heard Hunter suddenly cough once more and the sound was startlingly close. Then he heard the old man start cursing him, and when he was about halfway across the wash his name was yelled at him.

"Cameron! Hey you, Cameron!" Hunter called and afterward he waited a while. "Can't answer me, can you?" he asked the silence. Then after a moment more he said, "Blew the fool head clean off you with that last one, didn't I?"

Brooks moved on and after a few moments Hunter spoke again. "I got the money belt," Hunter boasted. "I got the breed, and now I got you." He laughed then, and his laughter, Brooks thought, was a chilling thing to hear. The wash echoed eerily with the sound.

Making his way up the far bank of the wash he heard the old man begin cursing him again, and he knew that Hunter must think he was lying up there dead, but was afraid to risk taking a look to make sure. When he reached the thicket at the top of the bank it was almost dark and the last of his strength was gone. He crawled a little way and then fell forward with his face on the rocks, and whether he slept or fainted he could not say. . . .

The stars were bright when he opened his eyes. The moon was high, and up the wash his bay horse was nickering. When the horse stopped, the brush whispered in a dry little breeze.

Where was Hunter?

Now his entire body was on fire, his tongue so parched and swollen it was difficult to close his mouth. He found a twig near his hand and he started chewing on it, trying to extract some moisture from it. He lay there looking at the moon shining down into the wash, and began to imagine he saw a shape moving there among the rocks. Several times he would have sworn he saw Hunter lurch from one rock to another, the bloody bandanna tied about one leg, a bloody hole in his chest and in the dry, murmuring sound of the brush he heard Hunter's whispered cursing, heard the echo of his cackling laugh.

During the rest of the night he sank several times into a kind of half-waking stupor.

At sunup he came fully awake, dragged himself to the edge of the thicket and looked cautiously out across the wash; then almost at once he whipped up his gun and fired. He fired all five cartridges in the chamber and afterward for a long, disbelieving moment he lay staring at what he saw. At last he got to his feet and started staggering down into the wash.

Hunter was in the crevice, sitting propped up there with his rifle resting on a rock and pointing at the thicket. Hunter was in the crevice, and Hunter was dead. He had been dead before Brooks started firing at him.

Chapter Sixteen

ALL ACROSS THE WASH he was aware of the glassy, staring eyes, the terrible gray mask of the face that looked down from the crevice. Twice on his way toward Hunter he stumbled and fell, and the second time he had to rest several minutes before he could get up and go on.

The first thing he did when he got up to the corpse was to snatch up the water bottle, tilt it and let the few swallows of brackish water it contained trickle down his throat. Hunter had Mr. Tilton's money belt, and he had the pouch of gold he had gotten for killing Willie. Brooks relieved him of those, then he dragged the body back into the crevice and threw some dead brush over it. While he was doing that he noticed a column of dust coming from the direction of the Tilton ranch.

When the buckboard passed along the road he was hidden in the brush. Hollis, the hand who had come out to stay with Jules, was driving the buckboard. He was looking toward the wash, as if he might have heard firing there, but he didn't drive over to investigate.

When the buckboard had passed, Brooks slid down into the wash again. He hid the money belt beneath some rocks close in near the bank, and put Jules's watch with it. Then he went staggering on along the trail to the place he had tied the bay horse, and the horse, hearing him coming, began neighing.

He had to stand leaning weakly against the horse for a while before he could untie him; then he laced his fingers in the mane and pulled himself up, hanging across the back of the bay for a minute like a sack of meal before he could get a leg over. Once astride, he lay forward, still clutching the mane. The horse turned out from the brush and automatically started back along the wash toward the Tilton ranch.

Lulled by the steady, rocking motion of the horse, he would doze and wake, and the journey seemed endless. Then he dreamed of water rippling over stones and he came awake once more to find the bay standing in the creek drinking. He slid off, got down in the meager ripples and feverishly scooped up the water with his hands. He put his face in the water, let it trickle down his burning throat.

Afterward he lay for a while in the shade beside the creek, then he got up and made his way around the corner of the house to the kitchen door. The door was open and Jules was standing just outside, looking down toward the corral. The bay horse, trailing the lariat, had come up to the corral and was standing there nudging at the poles of the gate.

After a moment Jules turned and saw Brooks, looking at him as if he were a ghost. He said a few words under his breath and crossed himself, and that gesture reminded Brooks of something, something that was very important, but he just couldn't seem to think what it was then.

"I need patching," he said. "Put some water on to heat." He followed Jules into the kitchen, placed his gun and the pouch of gold on the table and sat down heavily in a chair.

He sat and watched the Frenchman build up the fire. He stared at the pouch, the blood money Hunter had got for Willie, and what he was trying to think of had something to do with Willie.

"Put three pails on," he told Jules. "And bring out the tub. While that water's heating I could do with a mess of flapjacks and eggs."

By the time he had eaten, the water in the pails was steaming and Jules filled the big wooden tub. Jules had to pull off his boots for him, and then he got into the tub and soaked the bandages from the wound. The flesh around the hole was black and blue from the impact of the big slug, but the slug had gone on through, and there was no festering or swelling.

Jules got out the pain killer—a bottle of corn whisky with red Mexican peppers in it—and while Brooks stretched out on the table he poured some of the pain killer in the wound. Then he bandaged it with clean strips of cloth.

"When's Hollis due back?" Brooks asked.

"Tomorrow," Jules said. "He went to town to fetch a couple of hands. We got to pick the corn."

Brooks got off the table. "I'm going to bunk up a while now," he said. "If I don't wake by myself, you wake me before dark."

He took his gun and went down the hall past Mr. Tilton's room with its roll-top desk and four-poster bed, to his own room. He bolted the door behind him, made sure the bar was across the shutters on the window, then lay down on the corn-shuck mattress. And, though his weariness was like a weight pinning him down, he kept trying to think what it was that kept bringing Willie into his head. Then all of a sudden he knew what it was, and the certainty with which he knew made him sit bolt upright for a moment before he sank back.

He knew now that Willie hadn't been crossing himself like Jules did when Hunter asked him who had killed Mr. Tilton. Willie had been trying to make the outline of a star.

He woke, sweating in the airless room, his hand on the gun butt. He saw the silver of late afternoon light slanting through a crack in the shutter, then he heard Jules call his name again.

"All right," he said. "I'm awake."

He heard the cook leave his door and go back into the kitchen. He lay there, letting himself come fully awake. When he did get up he still felt weak from the blood he had lost, but he felt good. He got clean clothing from the chest of drawers and went out into the kitchen, instinctively wary as he entered, moving so soundlessly in his stocking feet that Jules gave a start when he turned from the stove and saw him.

Jules was fixing supper, and while Jules cooked Brooks shaved, and when his face was clean and smooth he wet a comb and slicked back his long mane of hair. He hadn't been so cleaned up since before they had hit the trail for Denver, and that seemed very long ago. Here it was fall already, roasting ears on the table and the ducks flying along the river on their way south.

Neither he nor Jules spoke until they had finished eating and had rolled cigarettes from Jules's tobacco. Then as they sat there in the last light, smoking and drinking their steaming mugs of coffee, Jules finally asked him the question that Brooks could tell he had been wanting to ask ever since his appearance that morning.

"The watch—" Jules said. "Is it all right?"

Brooks nodded. "You'll get it." He gazed at the cook, glad that he had the watch, that because of it he didn't have to worry about turning his back on Jules.

But there was another problem. He glanced at the pouch of gold coins that still lay on the table, and he saw that though Jules tried not to look at the pouch his eyes were constantly turning to it.

He tried to guess what Willie might have done with the money if he were alive and had it, but he could think of nothing, except that Willie would probably have given it away. He asked Jules finally where Willie was buried, and Jules said that when they wouldn't take him in the graveyard Gail Bull had made a grave for him on his place.

He'd get Willie a tombstone, he thought. Willie would like that. He'd get him the finest tombstone that money could buy, one with his name carved on it, and with the dates of birth and death.

He opened the pouch and counted out a hundred dollars and put it in his pocket. That would buy the tombstone. And now he didn't want the burden of disposing of the rest of the money. It was blood money, Willie's blood. He got up angrily and threw his cigarette end in the stove, then he took an old hat of Mr. Tilton's from one of the pegs by the door and put it on. He turned and stared at Jules. "I'm leaving that," he said harshly, pointing at the pouch. He waited for a moment. "Take it," he said then. "Keep it to go back to where you always been bellyaching to go." He opened the door and went out, and as he walked down toward the corral he felt relieved that he had no further responsibility in connection with that money. He hoped that Willie wouldn't mind what he had done.

Jules had put the bay horse back in the corral while he slept, and Brooks roped him, slid on him and rode back up the wash. It was dark, the stars were out and the moon was up again by the time he got to the place he had left the saddle; and, by then, he had thought everything through. Though when he first found the money belt it had seemed to him he was almost at the end of the trail, he realized now that he still had a long way to go.

He couldn't just ride into Tiltonville with the belt and tell people that Willie, when he was dying, hadn't crossed himself, as Hunter had supposed, but had actually been indicating the shape of a sheriff's star. If he was right, and it was Lufkin who had killed Mr. Tilton and then hidden the belt on his way back to town, he knew he was going to have to catch Lufkin with the belt on him in front of witnesses.

He was thinking about how he was ever going to do that as he saddled the bay. He thought about it as he rode on through the warm, moonlit night.

Coming down the north road it looked from the glare of light against the sky as if there must be a fire in the town. But after a while he heard the beating of a drum and he knew something was going on, maybe a troupe of players that had stopped off to put on a show, for the light in the sky came from flares.

When he reached the junction of the western road he could see that the flares were burning on either side of the courthouse steps and he caught a glimpse of the big drum. There were figures moving against the light and there was a crowd in front of the hotel. He could hear shouting and singing as he rode on across the river and came up along the south bank.

He tied the horse in the brush, just as he had before, and walked back across the river to wait for Mary, but after what had happened that other night he figured there was only a slim chance that she would be able to come. And now he had to see her; he had to tell her what he had figured out for her to do.

He was closer to the main street now and he could hear above the shouts and the singing a big, haranguing voice. He heard the name "Davis" several times and knew that the man was giving a speech, that it must be some political shindig that was going on.

After a while the speaker quit, but the noise didn't stop.

116

He could hear men going in and out of the bars, hoofs pounded along the street and now and then somebody fired off a gun.

She wouldn't come. By then he was certain of it, but he stayed on there in the cottonwoods until the moon passed behind the trees across the river and the noise along the main street died away to sporadic voices and the occasional sound of horsemen on their way home; then he started up the path she had fled along the other night. The path ran up around the back of the stage office, crossed the street where the shadows lay deepest beneath the plane trees, and lost itself in a lane that led up to the Reverend Ben Silk's barn.

A lamp was burning in the stage office, and as he came abreast of the lighted window he heard voices on the street.

"Dunk his head in the river," somebody said. "Just dunk his head—"

"Goin' down to the river," another voice sang. "Goin' down to the river to wash our sins away. Merril—you hear me? Keep the feet moving under that carcass of yours."

Three figures wavered in the light, then lurched abruptly from the street onto the path. One was the deputy named Kergan, a thin-faced, red-headed man with pale, bristling brows. He and another man Brooks had never seen before were supporting Merril Backus between them. All three were drunk, but Merril was the drunkest. As Brooks stood frozen in the shadow not more than ten feet away from them the trio paused. Kergan produced a bottle and handed it with a flourish to the other man, who was helping to support Merril.

"Merril, he don't need none," he said. As he spoke someone turned up the lamp in the stage office and Brooks realized that light now fell on the lower part of his body. He would have risked moving, but Kergan was already peering at him. "We got company," Kergan announced. "Step right over, pardner, and have yourself a drink."

Brooks held his breath a moment. "No," he said. He took out his bandanna and held it to his face.

"Best thing for what's ailin' you," the other man said. He extended the bottle.

117

Kergan laughed. "In the name of the law, stranger— take a drink."

Brooks shook his head, but he knew they could not see him do it. They could not see his face. Then he saw Kergan, in his mean, half-jesting mood, start to draw his gun. Before the deputy's hand could touch the butt he had drawn his own gun and the gun was entirely in the light where they could see it, see how steady it was. He did not speak again. After a moment he just waved the muzzle of the gun, prodding them on down the path.

He was gone from there almost as soon as they were, hearing them cursing behind him, and as he ran through the dust along the track of the blackest shadow there were two blasts and the slugs went tearing through the branches of the trees.

Then he was in the lane. He could see the lamps lit in the parlor of the Reverend Ben Silk's house. The parlor windows were opened against the warmth of the evening and after a moment he heard the blurred sound of Adam Lufkin's voice. Then there was another sound, and when he recognized what it was he was filled with a wild, raging fury. For the sound was of someone sobbing, and he knew that it must be Mary.

Chapter Seventeen

THERE WAS A CLUMP OF LILACS outside the parlor windows and, as he saw the deputy, Kergan, silhouetted, gun in hand, against the window of the stage office, he moved into the bushes, stepping carefully, parting the branches until he could see into the lamplit room. He could see the table with the crocheted cover, the big Bible lying on it, and the Reverend Silk standing by the table. Ben Silk was a short, wiry man in a black suit, with a broken nose, a frijole-colored complexion and pale, hairless head. Beyond her father he saw Mary. She was sitting on the sofa in a high-collared white dress. Her head was bent and her lovely face was covered by her fine, long hands. He could not see Lufkin, but his shadow, square and bull-like, was on the plaster wall.

"Heaven help you, girl!" the reverend was saying. "How can you hold back, how can you hesitate when a fine, God-fearing man is big enough to overlook what you done and still offer to take you for his wedded wife?"

Mary shook her head. "Please," she said, "I don't want to talk about it."

"You don't want to talk about it!" her father echoed angrily. "Well, we will talk about it! Do you deny it? Do you mean to sit there and deny you crept from this house in the night to go and meet with Joe Wood?"

Mary sobbed. "I don't deny anything," she said wearily. "Won't you please just let me be?"

"I come here for my answer," Lufkin broke in heavily. "I say I'll take you. I say Sunday."

Mary took her hands away from her face then and Brooks saw how pale she was. He could see the tears glistening on her lashes. And as she looked toward Lufkin he thought he had never seen her more beautiful. She looked so proud. "I'd never marry you," she told Lufkin.

There was silence for a moment, then Lufkin laughed, and suddenly the shadow on the wall loomed monstrous as he stood up. "Sunday," he repeated.

The Reverend Silk was gazing at Mary and now, Brooks thought he looked very tired and old. "Mary," he told her, "you go to your room."

Brooks watched her rise from the sofa, saw her walk through the doorway. He saw Lufkin move into the lamplight, gazing after her.

"Let her ma and me talk to her tomorrow," Ben Silk said wearily.

"It ain't every man'd overlook what I'm willing to," said Lufkin. "She and Cameron. Then Joe Wood. Preacher, it looks to me like she better marry me or else."

"Yes, Adam," the Reverend Silk said. "You're a good man. But I'm afraid the devil is in Mary."

Lufkin said, "It's up to you to get that devil out. That's your job, ain't it?"

"It is," the man agreed.

"By Sunday."

"Tomorrow's Friday," Ben Silk said. "That doesn't leave much time." He shook his head. "I dunno. Now I'm thinking maybe she ain't fit for so good a man as you, Adam."

"I'm sayin' I'll take her," Lufkin told him. His voice was rough and final, and after he spoke he stood staring at the older man.

"Yes, Adam," the preacher said.

"And Syd Tilton," Lufkin continued, "is going to stand up with me at the wedding. I told him it's for Sunday, and I don't think Syd would like it much if the wedding didn't come off and I was made to look foolish and to get laughed at around here." The sheriff paused, then added, "Especially since that church of yours is built on Tilton land."

This time the Reverend Ben Silk said nothing at all, and finally Lufkin picked up his hat. "Good night, Preacher," he said.

"Good night, Adam," the preacher told him.

Brooks heard the sheriff leave the house and go down the path to the street. He waited until Ben Silk turned out the parlor lamp, then he left the lilacs and went around the back of the house. He knew where Mary's room was, and the window of that room was dark. He went down to it, moving through the tree shadows, then leaning against the house and listening before he softly called her name.

"Brooks!" He saw the pale oval of her face at the open window, glimpsed her nightdress in the dimness of the room. "Be careful," she whispered. "Lufkin has somebody watching this house!"

"I waited for you," he said.

"It was killing me not to meet you. I was going to try to after a while. But I been thinking they might see me and follow—maybe find you."

He held her cool hands. "I got something to tell you."

"Please, darling, be careful," she whispered. "Please keep looking." She lifted one of his hands and pressed it quickly to her lips. "Brooks, take me away. Take me to California!"

He shook his head slowly, listening a moment, glancing toward the street. "I found Mr. Tilton's money belt," he said. "I got an idea Lufkin did that killing and hid the belt. Now I want to make him go for it."

"Lufkin!"

"You got to help."

"How?"

"Tell him," he said, "you'll marry him if he'll take you on a big, fancy wedding trip. Tell him you hanker to see New Orleans."

"I couldn't!"

"I don't mean you'll really go to do it." He gripped her hands. "If it is Lufkin, and I can prove it, then I can ride into this town again, ride up the street here in broad daylight—free. Nobody hunting me."

"Oh, Brooks," she said softly. "I'll do anything you say. But supposing I tell him I'll marry him and then supposing he don't go for the belt?"

"Just you tell him!"

She clutched his sleeve. "Listen—"

There was a sound of steps coming around the house, and as he heard the sound he tried to break free, but she dragged at him, her lips close to his ear. "In here!"

For an instant he hesitated, then he swung a leg up over the window sill. In the inner dark he shrank back against the wall, aware of the aroma of sachet from an opened drawer of the bureau behind him, hearing the steps come slowly along the side of the house. Outside the window the steps halted and now he could hear a man breathing, and smell tobacco and gun oil.

After a minute the man moved on around to the front of the house. They heard his steps on the porch, heard him knocking. A door opened down the hall. Steps went to the front door and it was opened.

As he heard the voices Brooks started to vault back out the window, but Mary held him, came up against him in her thin nightdress. "No," she whispered. "You're safer here."

The steps returned along the hall and stopped outside Mary's door. There was a knock and Reverend Silk called, "Mary—you in there?"

Mary waited an instant, then said in a sleepy-sounding voice, "What is it, Papa?"

The reverend said, "Your window's wide open. You got to close that window and keep it closed. You know all the riffraff that's come for this chivaree."

"All right," Mary said. She reached up and pulled the window shut.

"Don't open that window again," the reverend told her, and his footsteps went away.

Brooks bent and looked through the window as the man who had come to the front door and knocked left the porch. A match flared near the front of the house as the man lit a cigarette, and in the flare of the match he could make out the jowled, full face of the deputy, Gaines.

"I told you—" Mary whispered. "Lufkin has his people watching the place, to make certain I don't sneak out." She put her arms around his neck. "Brooks, I'm just so scared for you. If you found that money belt, why can't we just take it and go away? All I want is to be your wife —to be with you, not to have to lie awake worrying over you—never seeing you!"

"I'm telling you," he said fiercely. "I'm going to ride back into this town free, in the broad daylight. I'm going to, or I'll be dead. I'll do what I have to do!"

"I'm scared!"

"Better dead than hiding, moving at night. Better dead than scared to trust your own friends, fearing to show your face or to have your own name called."

Her lips touched his cheek. "I love you. I just can't think of anything else. I don't live for anything else."

He was silent a moment, listening to some men coming out of the hotel bar. Then he asked, "What's going on in town?"

"A big chivaree," she said. "It started today and goes on till Sunday. They got Davis people here to make speeches—senators and such. There's a dance tomorrow night. And Saturday night a big debate—the Davis men talking against the men for Coke. People from all over the county are coming into town for it."

"You got to tell Lufkin," he said. "See him in the morning, and tell him."

"I'll do whatever you say," she said. "I always will."

"Mary—" He held her to him, straining her close. "There's no other way. A man can't just think of himself. He's got to do what's right—right for everybody. And what's going on in Tilton County ain't right."

"I love you," she whispered. "I wouldn't love you half as much if you were any other way."

She was afraid to open her window again, and when he left he took his boots off and she opened her door and led him through the kitchen in the dark. She let him out the back door and for a long time he held her in his arms. It was so hard to leave her, because he never knew if he would see her again.

Chapter Eighteen

HE SPENT THE REST of that night in the wash near where he had rehidden the money belt, and in the first morning light he got Jules's watch out from among the stones where he had put it with the belt and rode on up the wash. When he got to the ranch house he tied the horse outside the kitchen door, cleaned up at the pump, and went into the kitchen to find Jules already cooking breakfast for him.

When he had eaten he rolled a cigarette and Jules fixed him a parcel of biscuits and meat. "Where do you ride now?" Jules asked him in a tentative, respectful way. "What do you do?"

He got up. "Going to set me a trap," he said. He gazed at Jules for a moment; then he got the watch out and laid it on the table. He turned on his heel and went out.

As he mounted, the kitchen door swung open again behind him and from the saddle he looked down at Jules standing there in the doorway with the watch in his hand and there were tears in the old man's eyes. "God ride with you," he said.

Then Brooks, to hide his sudden good feeling, told him grimly, "Take care you don't lose that Willie money in a seven-up game. You do, I'll see to it you never live to play again." He dug his heels into the bay, galloped across the creek, and turned up toward the wash.

An hour later, with the sun now well up, he tied the bay in some brush and pulled off the saddle. After that he went on along the wash on foot the half-mile or so to the area where Hunter's body lay and his own blood stained the rocks. He got the money belt again and put it in the place he had originally found it, then he made his way up into the thicket to wait.

As the day dragged on he felt he might wait there the rest of his life and no one would ever come. It might be that some total stranger had killed Mr. Tilton, hidden the belt and then gotten killed himself before he could return for it. The sun hung suspended in a burning, changeless sky, and now it all seemed like a long bad dream from that fateful Sunday on.

Across the wash he would think he saw Hunter's face again, a grinning death's-head rearing out from the brush. He would find himself listening intently, thinking he had heard Hunter coughing. Or he was in the jail again, waiting for them to come and lynch him. He was on the roan, fleeing south along the spine of hills. He was running, searching, hiding in the brush.

It was a dream and he was in it, but he could not see the end. The dream went on endlessly, and that afternoon was the longest part of all, a trail that never ended, a mirage on the plain near a town called Tiltonville, and there was a man who wanted to go back there, to return riding free, riding in the broad light of day for everyone to behold and speak his name.

As the afternoon waned he saw dust rising on the ranch road, a gray, moving plume coming from the direction of the town. After another half-hour he could make out the ranch buckboard. When it came abreast of the thicket, though still half a mile to the south of him toward the river, he could see the three men riding in it, and knew it would be Hollis and the two hands he had hired to help rick the corn.

As the buckboard passed, there was a distant rumbling above the plain behind him. He listened a moment disbelievingly, then he heard it again—thunder! He got up and threaded his way to the far side of the thicket where he could see out over the northern plain. When he saw the low black clouds on the horizon he couldn't believe it, either. It seemed so long since he had seen clouds.

By the time he got back to his place above the wash, the sun was behind the western hills. He knew there would be about an hour of clear, sunless light and perhaps half an hour of twilight. Would Lufkin come at night? Would he remember the hiding place well enough to find it at night?

He was thinking about that when his ears caught the sound of a horse coming up the wash. The horse was coming along slowly, raising no dust to mark its passage and that, he knew, could mean only that the rider—if the horse had one—sought concealment. There was no other reason for a rider to use the wash.

The horse did have a rider; above a low patch of brush he glimpsed his hat. Then abruptly horse and rider emerged from the brush and as he saw the man's face he swore softly to himself. It was not Lufkin. It was only Joe Wood.

He started to rise and call, then he noticed that Joe had stopped and was looking around. After a moment Joe rode on to the pile of stones where the money belt was hidden and got down. He looked carefully up the wash, and he stood quite still for a while, listening. Then he bent, pulled the stones aside and drew out the money belt.

Brooks watched him as he unfastened his shirt and trousers and strapped the belt around his waist. In stunned wonder he lay in the thicket and looked on, feeling that this surely was a dream, this day and all of it; then the blood began pounding in his ears and he felt sick. He felt worse than he had when Hunter shot him.

As Joe started to get back on his horse he crawled from the thicket and stood up at the edge of the wash. "Joe —" he called.

Joe whirled and saw him, and the hand which had fallen to his gun butt dropped slowly to his side. For a moment they gazed at each other. Then Brooks started down into the wash and Joe came toward him a few steps and stopped, waiting for him, and now that clean, cool, purplish light flooded the wash and the thunder, like buffalo guns, was rumbling again in the north.

When he was about fifteen feet away, Brooks stopped and Joe still had not spoken. He knew Joe was standing there wondering if he had seen what he had done, and finally he said to him, "Joe, you're getting kind of fat, aren't you?"

After a moment Joe said, "Maybe so."

"You better start to draw now, Joe," Brooks said. "We might as well get it over with." He waited. "Go on," he said. "Draw, Joe."

Joe shook his head. "No," he said.

Brooks studied the hard young face and the blue eyes

126

met his own squarely. "Do you want me to take you into town?" he asked him. "You know what they'll do to you there, don't you?"

"None of what you're thinking is true," Joe said.

"Don't give me that." Brooks dropped a hand to his gun. "Are you even too yellow to take a fighting chance? You want me to just shoot you down?"

"Sure," Joe said. "You can do that. Then you'd be worse off than you ever been. You'd kill your friend without waiting to hear him out. And if you was to go riding into town with the money belt on you who'd ever believe anything you said?"

Brooks stared at him. "Sure, friend," he said. "You killed Mr. Tilton and made certain it was going to look as if I did it. Then you aimed to run off with my girl. You told her we'd meet in Santa Fe. You told me Los Angeles. And you been saving your pay for the stage fare."

Joe had paled and now he said, stiff and white-lipped, "If that's what you're thinkin' maybe we better just shoot it out right now."

"What else can I think?"

Joe said slowly, "Maybe you forgot how you happened to leave that jail."

Brooks shook his head. "I haven't forgot. I just figure now your conscience was hurting you. And you wasn't ever expecting to see me around again."

Joe's face suddenly reddened. "You want me to draw now?" he asked grimly.

"You can talk first," Brooks said. "But I don't expect to believe anything you say."

"No," Joe said. "You won't. I'll just tell the truth of it, though. Then you can start shooting."

Brooks leaned back against a rock and crossed his arms, watching him. "Go on," he said. "Speak your piece."

Joe sat down on another rock. He brought out tobacco and papers and rolled a cigarette. When he had it going he said, "I found the money belt that day on my way back from talking to you up the river there. After listenin' to what you said I got to thinking how maybe it was somebody in the town who killed Mr. Tilton. I got to thinking if they didn't dare wear the money belt back there, what they would have done with it." He glanced over at the skeleton of the horse. "Seemed most likely they would have hidden that belt right around here," he said. "If they hid it."

Brooks gave a dry, mirthless laugh. "So you found it. And then you put it right back where it was."

Joe stared at him for a moment. "No," he said. "Where I just got it is where *I* put it. But that ain't the place I found it."

"Where did you find it?"

Joe pointed. "Right next to that dead wood behind you there. In them rocks."

Brooks did not turn his head to see. "Go on," he said.

"At first," he said, "I was going to take it and ride right back up the river and try to find you again. Then I figured to tell you about it when you came in to see Mary. The last thing I wanted to do was to carry that belt around. So I hid it in another place. Then riding on into town, I got to thinking."

Joe paused, took a sulphur match from his shirt pocket and relit his cigarette. "Like I told you that day," he went on. "I never figured you had a chance of ever provin' it on whoever it was that did kill Mr. Tilton. And finding the money belt, it seemed to me, was going to make it worse for you. What would you do with it? Nobody'd ever believe you didn't have it all the time."

"You figured to help me," Brooks said. "You just figured you'd keep that belt and save me trouble."

"Yes, I figured to help you," Joe said stonily. "And the best way I figured I could help was to get you away from Tilton County before you got killed and Lufkin got your girl, or before maybe she just up and died out of pure misery. I figured most of the money in this belt was yours, anyhow—all the back pay Mr. Tilton had been keeping for you. So I'd take Mary out to California. She could meet you there. Then I'd tell you about the belt."

"Sure!" Brooks said angrily. "In Santa Fe or Los Angeles. One place or another you'd meet me!"

Joe said calmly, "I seen Mary about sundown that night you rode in and I told her Santa Fe. Then between that time and the time I saw you down at the river I talked to the freighters and they told me about the herds makin' up along the Pecos." He took a slip of paper from the pocket of his shirt. "I got the name of that hotel written down here. I was goin' to ride on now and give it to Jules."

"Why?"

"To give to you if I couldn't find you."

Brooks frowned and reached up a hand, slowly pushing back his hat. "You ain't seen Mary?"

Joe shook his head. "I been out at the home place the last couple of days, saying good-by to my folks. On the way back to town I stopped to see Tarrant Smith and he said Lufkin was lookin' for me with murder in his eye, so I steered clear of town. Tarrant said the wedding was all set for Sunday and I figured the time had come to git. Tarrant was to tell Mary where to meet me tomorrow night. I figured to do just like I said when I talked to you."

"We ain't goin' to California," Brooks said.

Joe regarded him for a moment, then he reached inside his shirt, unfastened the money belt and drew it out. He rolled up the belt and threw it down in front of Brooks. "Well," he said. "I spoke my piece. That's all I got to say."

"Joe—" Brooks said. "What would you have figured? I was waiting here for the one that hid that belt to come for it." He paused. "And you came."

Joe thought for a while. "I reckon I'd of figured the same," he said finally. "I guess I don't blame you much."

The thunder had moved closer and now the wash was suddenly darkened as a cloud rolled over and lightning split the sky. "I been waiting for Lufkin to come for this," Brooks said, as the sound of the thunder passed. "Now I guess it wouldn't have done me much good if he had come." Along with his relief over Joe he was aware of a keen disappointment. If it was Lufkin, why hadn't he come?

Since there was about another hour of light remaining, he hid the belt where Joe said he had found it originally, then Joe led his horse up the wash, tied it, and joined him in the thicket to wait.

And now the thunder was like cannon on the plain, with a constant, flickering barrage to the north of them. Then they could smell the clean, sweet smell of the rain as it came. The rain came sweeping up the wash, pelted the thicket a few minutes, then passed on. And after that it quickly grew dark.

"He wouldn't come at night," Joe said. "Whoever it was, he wouldn't."

"He might."

"He wouldn't remember where he hid it—not in the dark. And it ain't as if he just put that belt there yesterday, either."

"He's got the bones of my cutting horse to mark where it was."

"In the dark you couldn't even see who it was that came to get it."

Brooks said, "That's what I was thinking. It would be better now to get the belt. If he comes at night and doesn't find it, he'll come back again by day."

"If he ever does come."

"He'll come," said Brooks. But he said it with a certainty he was far from feeling. Thinking about it now, it seemed remarkable anyone had left the belt there in the wash that long. Would Lufkin have? Would Syd Tilton? Who would—except perhaps a man who was dead? Could old Mr. Tilton, knowing he was followed that morning, have hid the belt on his way out to the ranch?

"Suppose it was Lufkin," Joe said. "You think you can buck that crowd. Even me—I can't show my face in Tiltonville now. When Lufkin's down on you he can pin anything on you. If he gets hold of me now I know what he'll do. He'll get Gaines to swear he recognized me as one of them that come in the jail that night and busted you loose. Then they'll hang me."

Brooks did not answer for a moment. Finally he said, "Let's get the belt."

"Give it up!" Joe urged him. "You and me might as well both say good-by to Tiltonville, and Texas."

"No," Brooks said. "I won't give it up."

"What about Mary? What about Sunday?"

Brooks got to his feet, and as Joe stood up he told him, "She won't marry Lufkin. I'll kill him first." He waited for a moment as thunder rolled along the wash. "Then we'll all take off for California," he said. It was the first time he had thought he might. If it had been Mr. Tilton who had hidden the money belt, he knew he might as well.

They got the belt and hid it in the thicket, and then they walked down the wash to where the horses were. Only when they were mounted and riding up out of the wash did Joe ask where they were going.

"Going to town," Brooks told him. "I got to see Mary. I got to find out if she told Lufkin what I said."

As they came up out of the wash it started to rain again and the two horses pranced and snorted and tossed their heads, behaving like a couple of colts. It rained hard for a while, drenching them; then the rain slacked off and settled down to a steady drizzle. When they hit the road they let the horses run and it was wonderful, just the smell of the dust, Brooks thought, as the rain fell on it, and the rain brought out the fragrance of the mesquite.

It wouldn't ever be the same elsewhere. All that the word home could ever mean, this was to him—this dust, this plain, the town, and the blackened, sentinel chimney west of town that marked the old home place. This was his identity in the world. Around the chimney he had hoped to build his home. Riding along through the rain he could see the kitchen. He could hear the rain beating on the roof, see Mary in the kitchen, wearing an apron, with her midnight hair done up, and flour on her hands.

When they came to the north road they turned in among some trees to get out of the rain for a while. They smoked a cigarette there, and then rode on. And as they went on toward the town Brooks had a feeling something big was going to happen, and he didn't know whether it was going to be good or bad.

"Joe," he said, "there's no real need for you to ride in."

Joe didn't answer for a while. Then, just when he began to think he hadn't heard, Joe said, "I figure you might need me."

From the way Joe spoke he felt that he too sensed something impending. Maybe it was only because of the rain, the sudden change it made, but he couldn't get over the feeling—the feeling everything was going to change, and change fast.

Chapter Nineteen

THE NIGHT WAS SO BLACK that they reined in at the junction without fear of being seen, sat their wet saddles with the rain dripping from their hatbrims, staring down along the main street, and the pulse of the big drum was beating through the rain. Tonight the flares were in front of the Trail Drivers' Hotel, hissing and sputtering, throwing a weird, garish light on the crowd gathered there on the walk beneath the wooden awning that ran along the hotel façade. The big hotel saloon was jammed and they could hear a babbling, softly roaring sound, like a mountain stream in the spring, and that was the sound of the crowd.

Then, as they sat there, there was another sound, the sound of music and organ notes, rain-muffled, rolling along the street to them. Presently voices began to sing the hymn, and they knew it must be Mary playing the church organ while the womenfolk had gathered there for a sing.

With her gone, Brooks thought, they wouldn't be watching the house. And after a moment he turned his horse, and Joe followed him up the muddy lane and round the black, looming shape that was the Reverend Silk's barn. They rode up the muddy plank ramp of the carriage entrance into the barn.

Brooks got down, smelling the musty, fragrant smell of the hay. He stood for a moment, listening. He could hear the cow in her stall and the whisper of the rain dripping down. He could still hear the noise from the hotel, but the organ had stopped. Men would be crossing the street, stopping at the church for their women. Mary and her parents would soon be home.

"I'm going to take a look," he told Joe.

Joe said in the darkness quietly, "I'll wait."

The faint glow of the turned-down lamp in the parlor fell on the lilacs, but there was no other light. He moved around the back of the house, feeling his way, passing the well and the stoop; he was standing by her darkened window. He put out a hand, felt the window and found that it was open a crack. Taking his time, he slowly opened it enough to admit him and swung up over the sill. He closed the window carefully, found a chair in the darkness and sat down—and now he felt abruptly strange. He sat there listening and waiting, and after a while he took off his hat.

He heard the voices, the steps of Mary and her parents making haste out of the rain up onto the porch, heard the Reverend Silk calling a final word to someone. Then they were in the house.

It was late. The drum had stopped, and he could hear them as they lit their candles, saying good night. He rose to his feet when he heard Mary's steps coming along the hall. She opened the door and he stood there with a warning finger to his lips, afraid she might cry out, but she did not. She stopped short just inside the door, recognizing him as the candlelight fell upon him; then she closed the door, blew out the candle and groped for his hands in the dark.

He could guess at her desperation just from the way she clung to him. "You have to take me away!" she whispered. "Take me away tonight!"

"What did Lufkin say?" He watched the window, saw the silver drops sliding down against the glow of the flares, and once more he had the feeling of events looming over him, about to topple down on him. He had to ask her again. "Did you tell him? What did he say?"

"He said he's got no money for any big wedding trip. He said we'd get married Sunday and take the stage for Austin. He's going to get a big job in the state government—maybe head of Governor Davis's own private police. Brooks—you have to take me away!"

"We have tomorrow," he said. He stroked her hair, thinking about the helplessness of the situation.

She whispered, "They're watching this house right now, and there'll probably be more watching tomorrow. Lufkin thinks Joe's coming back. He was questioning me. He thinks Joe and I might run off."

"What's on tomorrow night?"

"The big debate."

"Where'll it be?"

"In the schoolhouse, if the rain holds on."

"Tomorrow night will be better," he said then. "They'll all be there—the deputies, and Lufkin. They'll expect trouble at that debate." He said it, but that wasn't the reason he wanted to wait. He had to play it out to the end, wait until the ultimate moment before he gave it up. Then he would become what they said he was, a killer, because he would kill Lufkin. And he would be a thief, too, because he would take the money belt when he and Mary left.

She began to cry. "I can't endure it another day. Something will happen to you. I know it! You've strung your luck out too far already."

Yes, he thought, something will happen. Then he saw the light.

A lantern was moving along the side of the house, and he shrank back with her against the wall as the man carrying the lantern stopped by the window. The lantern moved closer to the window; then the light suddenly vanished as the man went on toward the rear of the house.

"What was he looking at?" Mary whispered.

"I must have left some mud on the sill," he said. "I guess that's what he saw."

"They know you're here, then."

"Maybe." He drew his gun. "You stay over there," he said. He led her to shelter beyond the dark bulk of the wardrobe. He could hear voices now out in back of the house and he no longer had any doubt the man with the lantern had seen signs of his entrance. But they wouldn't know who it was, he thought; they would think it was Joe Wood.

"I'm going now," he said quickly.

"No!" She held his arm. "I'm going with you! If you get killed, they can kill me too."

"Nobody's going to kill me," he said gently. "Mary—let me go."

She released him and he moved over to the door. There was a shout out in front of the house then and he heard steps on the porch. As he saw the lantern returning toward the window he opened Mary's door, crossed the hall and entered the darkened parlor. He heard Reverend Silk

134

come from his room, saw the flicker of his candle as he went to see who was at the door.

He slid a parlor window open and climbed out, dropping into the lilacs. Then a horse came galloping along the lane and he heard Joe yell, "Ki-hoo!"

Somebody behind the house shouted, "There he goes!" Then, as Joe reached the street, the man on the front porch fired.

Brooks moved through the lilacs to the edge of the porch just in time to see Joe in the light of the flares galloping full tilt past the hotel. There was another shot, and Joe's horse staggered and plunged to its knees. The horse rolled and screamed while Joe lay still, face down in the mud.

The man who had been on the porch ran out into the street. He fired again, killing the wounded horse. Then two more men came running from the other side of the house. They yanked Joe to his feet, and as he sagged between them, one of the men took his gun from him and hit him twice across the face with the gun barrel.

One of the flares suddenly hissed out. The other cast huge flickering shadows, lit the figures that had appeared from the hotel bar and the trio moving toward the doors. The one who had shot the horse followed, gun still drawn. That was Gaines, and one of those who supported Joe was the deputy, Kergan.

Brooks came out of the lilacs and ran toward the barn, stopping at the lamp to scoop up a handful of mud. He smeared the mud on his face and neck, then took his bandanna and wiped his eyes.

As he rode back along the lane he could see the dead horse in the guttering light of the one remaining flare; otherwise the street was empty. Then he was in the street himself; he was riding down the main street of Tiltonville once more—at night, with mud on his face and a cold, black fury in his heart.

When he came opposite the hotel entrance he turned the bay up onto the boardwalk under the awning, and reined in. And now he could hear, in the barroom, one big, angry voice above all the rest, and he knew who the voice belonged to. It was Sam Barron, a man who had been a friend of his father's, who also ranched on the western road.

"Turn him loose," Sam Barron said. "He's done nothing, nothing except to offend you Davis riffraff. All he's done is to be the son of Eli Wood, who was a confederate soldier. All he's done is to be a friend of Brooks Cameron."

"Watch your tongue, Barron!" It was Adam Lufkin's voice. "Watch what you say, or I'll lock you up."

"You!" Sam Barron said with fierce contempt. "You fat, carpetbagging feeder on the public. You, with your big, shiny star. You crook!" The voice was thundering now. "You don't belong in Texas! None of you do. And at the polls this time we'll throw you out!"

"Deputy Gaines," said Lufkin, "arrest that man!"

"Trying to capitalize on old Dave Tilton's murder!" Barron roared on. "If Dave Tilton himself should come in that door now he'd tell you just exactly what I'm telling you!"

Brooks dug his heels into the flanks of the bay and the horse sprang through the door, prancing and rearing there in the light of the big chandelier. He saw Joe, hatless and covered with mire, blood running down his face. Joe was slumped near the table where Lufkin sat, Lufkin looking like a king holding court. He saw Sam Barron and the group of ranchers who stood with him—and their hands had dropped on their guns as Gaines approached Barron. He saw the men from Austin in their long city coats standing at the bar, saw all this in the instant of his entry. Then in the sudden silence he could feel the mud on his face drying in the heat of the lamps, could feel it crack around his lips as he spoke.

"Joe—" he said. "Let's go." Joe's left arm hung limp, and his eyes when he looked toward Brooks were dazed. Brooks waited a moment, then he said again sharply, "Joe! Let's go."

Joe got up. He stuck out his right hand and grasped the table for support, and then started toward Brooks. At the same instant Kergan, with his gun half drawn, tried to grab him and use him as a shield, but before Kergan could touch him Brooks fired and the deputy reeled back against the table and fell.

As Joe came on, Brooks watched Lufkin. He knew that he would kill Lufkin now if he moved, but the sheriff kept his hands on the table and his heavy face was pale. He slipped his left boot out of the stirrup and gave Joe a hand up behind him, then he began backing the bay horse out the door, his eyes roving the room.

"Look along the street," he told Joe.

"All clear," Joe said.

He whirled the nervous, capering bay then and raced along the boardwalk a dozen yards before he turned out into the street, trying to keep the pillars that supported the hotel awning between them and the bar door. As they came to the stage office there were several shots. Then someone across the street fired at them.

He turned down to the fording and the river was high now, with the bay horse plunging through the muddy swells.

"Joe!" he said. "Joe—" He turned in the saddle. "You okay?"

Joe said faintly, "Sure."

"Hang on!" He unfastened the rope from the pommel and passed it around Joe's waist. "You been hit."

As Joe sagged against him he turned in the saddle and hung on to him while the horse labored up the bank. He swung sharply away from the morass of the road, keeping along the bank until they came to the shelter of some trees. He got down then. He slid Joe off, propped him against a tree trunk, and felt for the wound.

Joe's left arm was shattered above the elbow; he could feel the splinters of bone protruding. But there was more than that wrong with him. He had been hit, probably by the shot that had been fired at them from across the street as they passed the stage office. The bullet had entered the left side of Joe's chest and ranged through, leaving a jagged hole just beneath the right shoulder blade.

There were shouts from the direction of the fording now, a sound of horses on the road, but he paid no attention. He found a stick and began to tear strips from his shirt.

"You go on," Joe told him in a tired, blurred voice. "Take that money belt—take Mary. You go on."

Brooks laid the stick along the arm and bound the

137

strips around it. "You got a little nick in you," he said. "That's all. No worse'n a bad rope-burn."

"Leave me," Joe whispered.

"Just a bee sting," he said. "That's all. You're going to be fine."

He tore the rest of his shirt and bound it around Joe's chest and then, somehow, he got him back on the horse, coaxing, lifting and shoving him. When he had him in the saddle he climbed up behind him on the rump of the bay and they went on. He kept on along the bank for a while, then recrossed the river, heading for Tilton ranch.

"Old Jules will fix you up," he said. "He'll fix you up good as new. Nobody's better at patching and fixing than Jules."

He kept the bay horse plodding steadily through the night, through the cold, drifting rain; and all the while he talked to Joe, he kept on talking to him, but Joe never answered, and he didn't know if he heard. Joe sagged in the saddle with his head bent forward, his chin sunk on his chest.

Riding double that way, walking the horse, it took a long time to reach the ranch, and he thought it must be nearly morning by the time he crossed the swollen creek and rode up to the kitchen door. He leaned over and knocked on the door with his gun butt. After a moment Jules called out, asking who it was. Brooks told him. Jules lit a lamp then and opened the door. A lamp had gone on over in the bunkhouse too.

"Call and tell them it's all right," Brooks told Jules. He waited while Jules shouted to Hollis that there was nothing wrong and to get back to bed, then he got down and with Jules helping him he eased Joe from the saddle and carried him into the kitchen, but he knew as soon as he saw Joe's face in the lamplight that there was nothing they could do. Joe was dead.

Chapter Twenty

THERE WAS A CHILL, gray light seeping through the overcast as he rode back along the south bank of the wash, and now there was no longer a trail in the wash. The trail had become a miniature torrent, rushing to join the creek. After a few miles he crossed to the other bank and tied the horse in deep brush; then he went along on foot through the drifting rain until he came to the thicket where the money belt was. He got the belt and went down into the wash with it, putting it back beneath the stones where Joe had first found it.

Afterward he lay in the thicket, staring with burning, sleepless eyes into the misty, rain-drenched distance toward town, waiting for a rider to come.

All that morning he lay and watched the torrent in the wash, saw the muddy, foaming water rising inch by inch, creeping toward the banks, toward the stones where the money belt lay hidden. He knew that whoever had placed the belt there would come for it that day, if he was ever going to come.

Still the hours dragged on and there was nothing to break the chill, gray monotony of the afternoon, no sound but the rain dripping from the brush and the sound of the torrent. Then, finally, he had to struggle desperately to stay awake. He would find his eyelids drooping, his head would fall forward on his arms. He slept, even as he fought against it, and he dreamed that someone came for the belt, waking at last with a sense of panic to find that the day was nearly gone. Then he was about to go down to see if the belt was still there, when suddenly he saw the black silhouette of a man on horseback.

For a time the rider sat there, the rain glistening on his poncho while he looked carefully all about him. Then he rode down into the wash. He urged his horse across the swirling stream and dismounted on the other side. He was standing now just below the thicket, and when he turned his head Brooks saw that it was Lufkin.

Lufkin glanced back at the skeleton of the horse, as if to take his bearings from it, then he moved to the stones where the money belt was. He pulled aside the stones and lifted out the belt.

It was awful to have to lie there and watch Lufkin while he unfastened his poncho and his shirt and strapped the belt around his middle, but there was nothing else for Brooks to do. He had to play it out to the end. He was aware of a cold and passionless feeling of triumph; he knew that he had come to the last mile on that seemingly endless, perilous, will-o'-the-wisp trail that had beckoned him home.

He watched Lufkin remount, ride back across the stream and up the bank. He watched him ride into the gathering darkness toward town. When Lufkin had vanished he came out of the thicket and went for his horse.

He came down the north road on the tired bay horse, looked up the main street to see the flares sputtering in the rain; and he rode on across the fording, with the horse swimming at the middle. He knew they would be in the schoolhouse tonight for the debate, and he waited in the trees across the river where he could see the school. He saw the horsemen, the buggies, buckboards and wagons arriving. He saw the men entering the brightly lit school.

He waited until he knew the debate had begun. Then he put the bay into the river once more, crossed, with the horse swimming almost all the way, and rode up into the muddy schoolyard, the school where Mary, Joe and he had gone, where Willie Swallowtail had sometimes come to sit like a shadow at the back of the room.

He got down and tied the bay, moved along the wall until he came to a window. Then he could see the men sitting on the benches, with the aisle and the fat black stove dividing them. On the far side the Davis people sat —the carpetbaggers—and on the side nearest him were those who would vote for Richard Coke and a new day in Texas. He saw Sam Barron; he recognized others, the men who had been his father's friends. These were the men who had freed him from jail and whose cause he had all but ruined in Tilton County.

140

At the far end of the room Judge Kingston sat behind the desk, flanked on either side by three chairs in which sat the men who would carry on the Davis-Coke debate. One of the speakers on the Davis side was Lufkin, and he was the only man Brooks saw in the room who retained his gun and gunbelt.

Now, as he listened by the window, he could hear Judge Kingston speaking. The judge was saying that since everybody except Sheriff Lufkin and his deputies had parked their hardware at the door, he didn't expect trouble. He was warning everybody to behave and act like real gents. He thanked the distinguished visitors in the city coats for their presence, and then one of them on the Davis side got up and began making a windy speech, defending all Governor Davis had done. When that one finished talking a man on the Coke side got up and contradicted everything that had been said.

Brooks stood there waiting beneath the eave, gazing at the faces in the schoolroom, the ranchers with their work-scarred hands and clear, steady eyes, and he wanted only to be privileged to sit among them, free and clear. He waited there, gazing at Lufkin's face; waited until it should be the sheriff's turn to rise and speak, and when Lufkin did get to his feet and begin to talk he left the window and moved around the corner of the building, past the wagons and the horses tied at the rail, to the door.

At the Tiltonville school you went up two wooden steps onto a little porch where there was a foot scraper; then you went through the door into a long cloakroom with rows of pegs along the walls. Tonight, beneath the hats and ponchos, the pegs held gunbelts. Deputy Gaines was on guard, leaning against the jamb of the door that led from the cloakroom into the schoolroom. Gaines was looking into the room, listening to Lufkin, and he didn't hear Brooks.

Brooks jammed his gun in Gaines's ribs and said, "Step back!"

When he got Gaines around the corner in the cloakroom he turned him and hit him once with his fist, just for the good feeling it gave him, and as the deputy sagged he caught him and stretched him out on the cloakroom floor.

He took Gaines's gun, and with it in his left hand and his own gun in his right, he stood at the schoolroom door and stared once more at Lufkin—Lufkin in the bright light, with the star on his vest glittering, his pale eyes, his heavy face like dough, while the satisfied, nasal sound of his voice went rolling about the room. Lufkin was talking; Lufkin was bragging about himself.

A head turned. Someone saw him standing there at the door with his guns. More heads turned and a whisper ran along the benches.

"You take the case of Mr. Dave Tilton's killing—" Lufkin was saying. "I remember the day that sneaking, murdering Brooks Cameron rode back here after he done it."

Lufkin stopped talking abruptly and in the taut, electric silence that had fallen upon the room he stared, squinting against the light, peering down the aisle at Brooks.

"You mentioned my name," Brooks said, finally. "But I didn't kill Mr. Tilton." He waited for a moment, his eyes on Lufkin's hands. "The man who killed Mr. Tilton," he went on, "is wearing the money belt that belonged to him right now." He waited another long moment, then said, "Sheriff, I'm going to ask Mr. Sam Barron to step up there and see if you might be the man."

Sam Barron rose from his bench. He hesitated for only a moment, then moved slowly toward the front of the room. And now Brooks could see the sweat standing out on Lufkin's face.

Barron stopped two paces from Lufkin and said, "Turn around, Sheriff."

Lufkin turned, but as Sam Barron moved to him and stabbed with probing fingers at his waist, the sheriff whirled and grabbed him, held him as a shield, and at the same time whipped out his gun and fired. The bullet hit the stove, ricocheted, and went screaming into the roof. Benches were overturned as the men on them hit the floor.

Brooks did not move. He stood there with a curious feeling of detachment, watching Lufkin, holding his fire. Lufkin shot wildly once more as he dragged Barron with him toward a window, then he sent the rancher reeling with a blow, there was a crash of glass and Brooks turned, sprang through the cloakroom and down the steps.

He glimpsed Lufkin running up toward the line of horses, but he could not fire because of the horses. Then Lufkin, seeing him, turned and lurched through the mud toward the river and the trees.

He fired, and fired again. He saw Lufkin slip and fall forward into the trees and he ran on into the blackness and the rain, hearing now the shouts behind him, the booted feet rushing from the school.

Among the trees there was the sound of the river, and there was also a sodden sound of movement in the brush underfoot. He could see nothing until he reached the river, and then, cutting across the surface of the water, he glimpsed the head of a man and he plunged on after him.

In the river the water pulled at him and suddenly, quite close, he saw the pale blur of a face and he dived for it. He felt a massive arm encircle his neck and he smashed at the face with his fists until the force of the arm lessened, then his fingers were at Lufkin's throat and Lufkin's thumbs were locked upon his throat, pressing the life from him, dragging him down. . . .

A good many of them stayed in the schoolhouse that night, and when Brooks woke it had stopped raining. He was lying wrapped in a buffalo robe and someone had hung his clothes to dry.

Sam Barron was talking to some men, and when he saw that Brooks was awake he said, "Welcome back to Tiltonville, Brooks Cameron."

Brooks sat up. He looked around the familiar schoolhouse and finally said, "It took some doing to get back." He stared at the early sun streaming through the windows, remembering riding through the rain with Joe, remembering Willie slung over a saddle.

"Lufkin—" he said, looking inquiringly at Sam.

Sam brought him a cup of coffee. "That's one killing nobody'll ever lynch you for," he commented.

Brooks stood up and looked out the window. It was still the fair land Mr. Tilton and his grandfather had come to after the wars, but he knew the changes in it. Once he'd seen the buffalo, massed black on the prairie as far as the eye could see; he'd traveled the prairie and seen the white, bleached cities of bone. The buffalo were gone, along with their hunters. And his own youth was behind him.

Sam Barron asked, "Was it you rode into the hotel barroom after Joe?"

Brooks nodded, and began to dress.

"How's Joe?"

"Dead," Brooks said. . . .

The morning was beautiful after the spell of rain; it was another Sunday morning and the bell of the New Freedom Church rang as Brooks got down in front of the Reverend Silk's house. He tied his horse at the hitch post and as he started up the walk the front door opened and Mary stood there in a white dress, looking like a dream. He saw the tears shining in her eyes, and he thought, "I've done it. I've come to the end of the trail. I've come home."